The
ESSENTIAL COLLECTION

Shipment Five

Rainy Day Kisses
Mail-Order Bride
The Matchmakers
Father's Day
A Friend or Two
No Competition

Shipment Six

First Comes Marriage
White Lace and Promises
Friends—and Then Some
The Way to a Man's Heart
Hasty Wedding
That Wintry Feeling
Those Christmas Angels

Shipment Seven

Borrowed Dreams
Starlight
Promise Me Forever
Shadow Chasing
For All My Tomorrows
The Playboy and the Widow

Shipment Eight

Fallen Angel
Yesterday's Hero
Reflections of Yesterday
All Things Considered
The Trouble With Caasi
Almost Paradise

The
ESSENTIAL COLLECTION

#1 *New York Times* Bestselling Author

DEBBIE
MACOMBER

Navy Woman

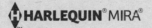

Recycling programs
for this product may
not exist in your area.

ISBN-13: 978-0-373-47280-2

NAVY WOMAN

Printed in U.S.A.

DEBBIE MACOMBER

is a number one *New York Times* and *USA TODAY* best-selling author. Her books include *1225 Christmas Tree Lane, 1105 Yakima Street, A Turn in the Road, Hannah's List* and *Debbie Macomber's Christmas Cookbook,* as well as *Twenty Wishes, Summer on Blossom Street* and *Call Me Mrs. Miracle.* She has become a leading voice in women's fiction worldwide and her work has appeared on every major bestseller list, including those of the *New York Times, USA TODAY, Publishers Weekly* and *Entertainment Weekly.* She is a multiple award winner, and won the 2005 Quill Award for Best Romance. There are more than one hundred million copies of her books in print. Two of her Harlequin MIRA Christmas titles have been made into Hallmark Channel Original Movies, and the Hallmark Channel has launched a series based on her bestselling Cedar Cove series. For more information on Debbie and her books, visit her website, www.debbiemacomber.com.

Dedicated to
Betty Zimmerman
A remarkable woman and a very special aunt

Special thanks to
Cheryl K. Rife, LCDR, JAGC, USN

One

Rain. That's all it had done from the moment Lieutenant Commander Catherine Fredrickson, Judge Advocate General Corps—JA6C—arrived at the Naval Submarine Base Bangor in Silverdale, Washington. October in Hawaii meant balmy ocean breezes, *mai tais* by the pool and eighty-degree sunshine.

In other words she'd left paradise and had been transferred to purgatory.

If the weather wasn't enough to discourage her, the executive officer, Commander Royce Nyland was. Catherine had never met anyone who irritated her more. The legal staff stationed in Hawaii had shared a camaraderie that made working together a pleasant experience.

Bangor was a different story, but the contrast was most telling in the differences between Catherine's two superiors. She simply didn't like the man, and from all outward appearances the feeling was mutual.

From the first, Catherine knew something wasn't right. In no other station had she been required to stand duty so often. For four weeks straight she'd been assigned the twenty-four-hour watch on a Friday night. It was as if Commander Nyland had made it his personal goal to disrupt her entire life.

After a month, Catherine was getting downright testy about it.

"Fredrickson, do you have the files on the Miller case?"

"Yes, sir." She stood, reached for the requested file and handed it to the man who'd been dominating her thoughts for the majority of the day.

Commander Nyland opened the file and started reading as he walked away from her. Catherine's gaze followed him as she tried to analyze what it was about her he disliked so much. Perhaps he had something against brunettes. Although that sounded crazy, Catherine couldn't help wondering. Maybe it was because she was petite and small-boned. More than likely, she reminded him of someone he once knew and disliked intensely. Well that was just too damn bad. As far as Catherine could see, she'd done nothing to deserve his disdain, and frankly, she wasn't about to put up with any more of it.

Scuttlebutt had it that he was single. Catherine had no trouble believing it. If his behavior toward her was any indication of how he treated women, then this guy needed a major attitude adjustment.

His apparent dislike of her solved one problem. Catherine needn't worry about anything romantic developing between them. If she were looking for an effective way to end her Navy career, all she had to do was start fraternizing with a superior officer within the same command. It was the quickest way Catherine knew to be court-martialed. The Navy refused to tolerate such behavior.

Besides his rotten attitude, Commander Nyland wasn't her type. Catherine liked her men less rough around the edges and a whole lot more agreeable.

In eleven years of Navy life, Catherine had worked with her share of officers, but no one had ever struck such a strong, discordant note with her.

Nothing she did pleased him. Nothing. The closest she'd ever gotten to praise from her XO had been a hard nod, as if that were sufficient compliment. A nod!

The crazy part of it was, Catherine had actually gotten excited over it. All day she'd gone around wearing a silly grin.

She needed to get back to Hawaii, and fast.

"Come into my office, Lieutenant Commander."

Catherine glanced up, startled to discover Commander Nyland standing directly in front of her desk.

"Yes, sir," she answered briskly. She stood and reached for a notepad before following him into his office.

Commander Nyland took his seat and motioned for Catherine to sit in the cushioned chair located on the opposite side of his desk.

Catherine glanced around and swallowed nervously. She didn't like the looks of this. The great and almighty commander was frowning. Not that it was the least bit unusual. To the best of her memory, she couldn't remember him ever smiling.

She quickly reviewed the cases she'd been working on for the past few days, and could think of nothing that would warrant a tongue-lashing. Not that he needed an excuse, of course.

The silence stretched to uncomfortable lengths as she waited for him to acknowledge her. It was on the tip of her tongue to remind him he was the one who'd called her into his office, but she'd be a fool to allow a hint of sarcasm into her voice.

"I've been following your progress for the past several weeks." His indifferent blue gaze raked her features. Catherine had never been more aware of her appearance. Her thick, dark hair was coiled in a businesslike knot at her nape, and her uniform jacket and skirt were crisp and freshly pressed. She had the impression if he found one crease, she'd be ordered to stand in front of a firing squad. No man had ever made her feel more self-conscious. He continued to stare at her as if seeing her for the first time. There was no hint of appreciation for her good looks. Catherine wasn't conceited, but she was reasonably attractive, and the fact the man looked at her as if she were little more than a mannequin was vaguely insulting. Okay, she was being unreasonable, Catherine mused. If she had recognized a flicker of interest in those cobalt-blue eyes of his, that would have been worse.

"Yes, sir."

"As I was saying," he continued, "I've had my eye on your work."

She noted that he made a simple statement of fact without elaborating. If he'd been watching her, then she'd admit, not openly of course, that she'd been studying him, too. He may be disagreeable, and to her way of thinking, ill-tempered, but he was respected and generally well liked. Personally, Catherine found him to be a real pain, but her thinking was tainted by a four-week stint at standing duty on Friday nights.

Politics existed in every office, but there seemed to be more in Bangor than the other duty stations Catherine had been assigned. As the executive officer directly below Captain Stewart, Commander Royce Nyland was empowered to run her legal office. He did so with a detached, emotionless ability that Catherine had rarely seen. In many ways he was the best officer she'd ever worked with and, in others, the worst.

It was apparent the man was a born leader. His lean, muscular good looks commanded attention. His office demanded it.

Actually, now that she had an uninterrupted minute to analyze the commander, she was willing to admit he was fairly attractive. Not handsome in the classic sense. Appealing, she decided. Not ordinary.

His features weren't anything that would cause a woman to swoon. His hair was nearly black. Its darkness coupled with his deep blue eyes was a contrast not easily ignored. He was broad-shouldered, and although she knew him to be of medium height, an inch or so under six feet, he gave the impression of power and strength in everything he did.

Her scrutiny didn't seem to bother him. He leaned back in his chair, expelled his breath and announced, "I'm pleased to tell you I've chosen you as a substitute coordinator of the physical fitness program for the base."

"Substitute coordinator," Catherine repeated slowly. Her heart beat dull and heavy before it dropped like a lead weight to her stomach. It took a second to right itself before she could respond. If there was one after-hours duty she would have done anything to avoid it was that of coordinator of the physical fitness program. It was by far one of the least envied jobs on base.

The Navy was serious about keeping men and women in top physical condition. Those who were overweight were placed on a strict dietary schedule and exercise regime. As coordinator, Catherine would be subjected to endless meetings to chart the individuals' progress. She'd also be expected to formulate an exercise program designed specifically to meet each person's needs. In addition, she would be given the painful task of having someone discharged from the Navy if they failed to meet the requirements in regard to weight and fitness.

"I believe you're qualified to handle this job effectively."

"Yes, sir," she said, biting her tongue to keep from saying more. Tackling this duty, even on a substitute basis, meant she wouldn't have time to breathe. It was a time-consuming, distasteful assignment. If the executive officer had been actively seeking to destroy any chance she had of developing a social life, he'd done so in one fell swoop.

"Lieutenant Osborne will meet with you and give you the necessary paperwork at 1500 hours. If you have any questions, you should gear them to him." Already he was looking away from her, dismissing her.

"Thank you, sir," she said, struggling with everything in her not to let her irritation show. She left his office and closed the door with a decided click, hoping he'd believe the wind had caught it. Hell, he was fortunate she didn't tear the damn thing right off its hinges.

With as dignified a walk as possible, she returned to her office. She set the pad down a little too hard, attracting the attention of Elaine Perkins, her secretary, who occupied the scarred desk outside Catherine's office.

"Problems?" she asked. As a Navy wife, Elaine was well acquainted with the difficulties of military life.

"Problems?" Catherine echoed sarcastically.

"What could possibly be wrong? Listen, do I have something repugnantly wrong with me?"

"Not that I've noticed," Elaine was quick to tell her.

"I don't have bad breath?"

"No."

"Does my slip hang out from under my skirt?" She twisted around and tried to determine that much for herself.

"Not that I can see," Elaine assured her. "What makes you ask?"

"No reason." With that, Catherine stalked out of the office and down the hall to the drinking fountain. Her hand trembled slightly as she leaned forward and scooped up a generous mouthful, letting the cold water soothe her injured pride.

Catherine wished she could talk to Sally. The two were the only women officers in a command of several hundred men, but that wasn't possible now. Once she'd composed herself sufficiently to return, Catherine did so, forcing a smile.

"I'm *pleased* to inform you you've been chosen as the substitute coordinator of the physical fitness program," Catherine mumbled under her breath as she traipsed toward the running track several hours later. Dusk was settling over the compound, but there was enough time to get in a three-mile run before dark.

Pleased was right. Commander Nyland had looked downright gleeful to assign her the task. The more Catherine thought about it, the more furious she got.

Venting some of this discontent seemed like a good idea. Clouds threatened a downpour, but Catherine didn't care. She'd just received the worst collateral duty assignment of her career, and she needed to vent the frustration and confusion before she headed home to the apartment she rented in Silverdale. Taking giant strides, she crested the hill that led to the track, then stopped abruptly. Several runners circled the course, but one runner in particular stood out from the rest.

Commander Nyland.

For a long moment Catherine couldn't keep her eyes off him. There was a natural, fluid grace to his movements. His stride was long and even, and he ran as if the wind were beneath his feet. What struck her most was his quiet strength. She didn't want to acknowledge it. Nor did she wish to find a single positive attribute about this man.

If there was any justice in the world, lightning would strike him dead. Glancing to the sky, she was depressed to note a touch of blue in the far horizon. Typical. Just when she was looking for rain, the sun had decided to play a game of hide-and-seek with her. If lightning wasn't going to do the good commander in, then all she could hope for was a bad case of athlete's foot.

Once again she grumbled under her breath, seriously considering leaving the base without running. If she did go down to the track, it was likely she'd say or do something that would get her into trouble with the commander.

Evidently she'd done something horrible to warrant his dislike. After he'd ruined four week-ends straight for her, he'd topped himself by giving her the least desirable assignment on base. What next? KP?

Catherine started to turn away, then abruptly changed her mind. She wasn't going to allow this man to dictate her entire life! She had as much right to run on this track as anyone. If he didn't like it, he could be the one to leave.

With that thought in mind, she stepped alongside the court and went through a series of warm-up exercises. Actually, the more she thought about it, she was downright eager to get onto the track. She was petite, but she was a fine runner. She'd been on the varsity cross-country teams in both high school and college and did a consistent seven-minute mile. If there was an area in which she excelled, it was running.

She did the first lap at a relaxed pace, easily lapping a couple of the overweight men. Commander Nyland didn't acknowledge her one way or the other, which was perfectly fine with Catherine. She'd hadn't come out here to exchange pleasantries with him.

The second and third laps, Catherine stepped up her pace. It normally took her a mile or so to fully warm up. As she increased her stride, she noticed that she was never quite able to catch her XO.

The one time she did manage to pass him, he scooted past her seconds later, leaving her to eat his dust. Frustrated, Catherine decided she might not be able to outrun him, but by heaven she'd outlast him. He was fast, but she'd easily outdistance him.

She continued her killing pace until she was sure she'd gone six miles or farther. Her lungs ached, and her calf muscles strenuously protested the abuse. Yet she continued, more determined than ever not to surrender her pride to this disagreeable commander. If she was hurting, then so was he.

She would rather keel over from exhaustion than quit now! It was more than a matter of pride.

Soon fat raindrops fell from the darkening sky and splashed against the dry, gritty surface. Still Catherine and the commander ran. What few runners remained quickly dropped out until it was the two of them alone against the forces of nature. Against each other, in a silent battle of wills.

They didn't speak. Not once. Catherine ran until she thought she was going to be sick, yet she dared not stop. Night fell like a curtain of black satin around the grounds. Catherine barely managed to see her own feet, let alone the distant silhouette of the commander. Soon he disappeared from her range of view entirely. It wasn't until she heard his footsteps coming up behind her that she realized he'd been able to come all the way around to lap her. He slowed his pace until his steps matched her own without breaking his stride.

"How much longer are we going to keep this up, Fredrickson?" he demanded.

Damn, he didn't even sound out of breath, Catherine noted.

"I don't know," she returned, sounding very much as though she should have yielded several miles back.

"You're tiring."

How kind of him to tell her so. "You are, too," she insisted.

"I have to admit you're a hell of a runner."

"A compliment, Commander?"

She sensed his smile. It made absolutely no sense the way her heart reacted knowing that. It was as if she'd been blessed by an unexpected second wind. By some odd twist of fate, she'd actually managed to amuse ol' stone face.

"Don't let it go to your head."

"No chance of that," she quipped, wondering if she'd heard a hint of amusement in his tone. "I don't suppose you happened to notice it's raining." Although she attempted to make light of it, she was drenched to the bone.

"Is that what all this wet stuff is?"

"I'll tell you what," she said between breaths, "I'll stop running if you do. We'll call it a draw."

"Agreed." Royce slowed his pace to a trot, and Catherine reluctantly did the same, not sure even now that she could trust him. After several steps, she stopped and leaned over, bracing her hands on her knees while she struggled to capture her breath.

The rain continued to pound down with a vengeance. While they were jogging, it was a simple enough matter to ignore the downpour. Now it wasn't so easy. Her hair, which had once been neatly secured at her nape, was plastered to her cheeks like wet strings. A small river of rainwater was navigating over her neck and down to the small of her back.

"Go home, Fredrickson," Royce said after a moment.

Catherine bristled. "Is that an order?"

He paused. "No."

He started to walk away from her, then unexpectedly turned back. "Before you leave, satisfy a curiosity. You requested a transfer from San Diego several years back. Why?"

Catherine knew it was all part of her personnel file, but his question caught her off guard. Her response was quick, light-hearted, almost flippant. "Who wouldn't want to live in Hawaii?"

"That wasn't the reason you wanted out of San Diego." His voice was deceptively unconcerned, as if he knew far more than he was letting on. "You wanted that transfer and you didn't care if you got Hawaii or Iran."

"There were personal reasons," she admitted reluctantly. Catherine couldn't understand why he'd chosen to ask her these questions now. The man continued to baffle her.

"Tell me the truth."

Catherine tensed, disliking his casual tone. Nor was she pleased with the way he implied she was lying. By mentally counting to ten, she willed herself to remain calm.

"That is the truth. I've always wanted to live in Hawaii."

"My guess is that a man was involved."

Catherine's stomach knotted. She didn't often think about Aaron. For the past three years she'd done a superb job of pretending they'd never met. Leave it to Royce Nyland to harass her battered heart with memories of her former fiancé. All right, that was a bit strong. He wasn't exactly tormenting her, and her heart wasn't all that scarred.

"What makes you think my request had anything to do with a man?" she asked, making light of his comment. She increased her strides, wanting to get this interrogation over with as soon as possible.

"Because it generally is."

That wasn't the least bit true, but Catherine wasn't going to stand in the rain and argue with him.

"A change of scenery appealed to me at the time." She needed to get away from San Diego for fear she'd run into Aaron. She wouldn't have been able to bear seeing him again. At least that was what she told herself. Over time, she wasn't nearly convinced that was true. She'd fallen head over heels in love with him much too quickly. Then she'd flown out as a defense attorney for trials aboard the *Nimitz* and returned several weeks later to learn Aaron hadn't exactly been holding his breath waiting for her.

The first minute she was back, Catherine had rushed to her fiancé's apartment to find him lying on the sofa with the young blond divorcée who lived next door. Aaron had scrambled off the davenport in a rush to explain while the red-faced divorcée hastily rebuttoned her blouse. It had all been innocent fun, Aaron claimed. Hell, how was he supposed to amuse himself while she was away for weeks on end? He advised Catherine to be a sport since he and the blonde had only indulged in a little entertainment.

In thinking back over the episode, Catherine was surprised by how completely emotionless she'd remained. The solitary diamond on her finger suddenly weighted down her hand. That much she remembered with ease. She'd stared down on it and then wordlessly slipped it from her finger and returned it to Aaron. For several moments he was paralyzed with shock. Then he'd followed her to the parking lot and pleaded with her to be more understanding. If it offended her so much, he'd make sure it didn't happen again. There was no need to overreact this way. None whatsoever.

In retrospect Catherine had come to realize that her pride had taken far more of a beating than her heart. She was almost relieved to have Aaron out of her life, only she hadn't realized that until much later.

"Catherine?"

Royce's deep, masculine voice pulled her back into the present. To the best of her knowledge it was the first time he'd ever used her name. Until then it had been Lieutenant Commander or Fredrickson, but never Catherine. This, too, had a curious effect upon her heart.

"There was a man involved," she announced stiffly, "but that was several years ago now. You needn't worry my former engagement will affect my work for you. Now or in the future."

"I'm pleased to hear it."

"Good night, Commander." They crested the hill where Catherine's bright red GEO Storm was waiting for her.

"Good night."

Trotting, Catherine was halfway down the hill when Royce stopped her.

"Catherine."

"Yes?" She turned around to face him, brushing the wet curls from her cheeks.

"Are you living with someone?"

The question took her by complete surprise. "That's none of your business."

Royce said nothing. He stood several feet away from her, his harsh features illuminated by the streetlight. His face was tight, as if he were holding himself in check. "Trust me, I have no interest in your love life. You can live with whomever you please or be engaged to five men at once for all I care. What does concern me is the legal department. The work is demanding and the schedule grueling. I like to know where I stand with my staff and try to avoid causing unnecessary complications in their lives."

Catherine didn't respond right away. "Since you find it so important, then I might as well confess I am shacked up with someone." From the distance Catherine couldn't tell if she got a reaction or not. Most likely he was telling the truth and he didn't care one way or the other. "Sambo."

"Sambo?" he repeated frowning.

"You heard me correctly, Commander. I live with a cat named Sambo." With that, she gave a cheerful laugh and was gone.

Royce found himself smiling in the dark, the rain pelting down around him in a great torrent. His amusement, however, vanished quickly. He didn't like Catherine Fredrickson.

"No," he muttered aloud, retracting the thought. That wasn't true. He did like her. There were any number of admirable traits about the Lieutenant Commander he couldn't help but respect.

She was dedicated and hardworking, and she'd fit in easily with the rest of his staff. She wasn't a complainer, either. Before he'd left the office that evening, he'd checked over the duty roster and was surprised to note that he'd assigned Catherine duty every Friday for four weeks running. He hadn't realized his mistake. Anyone else would have pointed it out to him, and rightly so. Her name had drifted easily into his mind when he learned Lieutenant Osborne was going on sea trials and a substitute coordinator was needed to take over the physical fitness program.

He knew Catherine wasn't overly pleased by the assignment. Her eyes had flashed briefly with rebellion, but that was the only outward sign she'd given that she wasn't thrilled with the added responsibility.

That woman had eyes that would mark a man's soul. Normally Royce didn't pay much attention to that sort of thing, but her eyes had garnered his attention from the first moment they'd met. They shimmered, and seemed to trap pieces of light. But more than that, they seemed warm and caring.

He liked her voice, too. It was rich and sweetly feminine. Female. Hell, Royce mused, he was beginning to sound like a romantic poet.

Now that thought was enough to produce a hearty laugh. There wasn't a romantic bone left in his body. His wife had squeezed every ounce of love and joy out of him long before she went to the grave.

Royce didn't want to think about Sandy. Abruptly he turned and walked toward his car, his strides hurried, as if he could outdistance the memory of his dead wife.

He climbed inside his Porsche and started the engine. His house was on the base, and he'd be home within five minutes.

Before long, however, it was Catherine who dominated his thoughts again. He wasn't overly thrilled with the subject matter, but he was too damn tired to fight himself over it. When he arrived home, his ten-year-old daughter, Kelly, would keep him occupied. For once he was going to indulge himself and let his thoughts wander where they would. Besides, he was curious to analyze his complex reaction to Catherine Fredrickson.

Not that it was important. Not that he needed to know anything more about her than he already did. He was simply inquisitive. He supposed when it came right down to it, he didn't feel one way or the other about her.

No, that wasn't true, either. She intrigued him. He didn't like it. He didn't understand it. He wished he could put his finger on exactly what it was about her that fascinated him so much. Until that afternoon, he hadn't even been aware of it.

She wasn't that much different than the other Navy women he'd worked with over the years. Not true, he contradicted himself. She had a scrubbed-clean look about her, a gentleness, a gracefulness of heart and manner that piqued him.

Another thing he'd learned about her this evening. By heaven that woman was bullheaded. He'd never seen anyone run with cursed stubbornness the way she had. It wasn't until it had started to rain that Royce recognized the unspoken challenge she'd issued. Absorbed in his thoughts, he hadn't noticed she was on the track until she'd zoomed past him and then smugly tossed a look over her shoulder as if to announce she'd won. Hell, he hadn't even realized they were in a race.

As if that wasn't enough, she wouldn't stop. They both had reached their physical limits, and still that little spitfire continued and would have, Royce was convinced, until she dropped.

He pulled into the driveway and cut the engine. His hands remained on the steering wheel as a slow smile spread across his features. *Woman*, he mused, *thy name is pride*.

The drape parted in the living room, Kelly's head peeked out. Just the way the drape was tossed back into place told him the ten-year-old was angry. Damn, Royce wondered, what the hell had he done this time?

Kelly usually ran outside to greet him. Not tonight. Whatever it was must have been a doozy. His daughter could be more stubborn than a Tennessee mule. This must be his day for clashing with obstinate women.

Two

Fresh from the shower, Catherine dressed in a warm robe, and wrapped her hair in a thick towel. She sat in the living room, her feet propped against the coffee table with Sambo nestled contentedly in her lap.

Sipping from a cup of herbal tea, Catherine mulled over the events of the day. A reluctant smile slowly eased its way across her face. Her dislike for Royce Nyland didn't go quite as deep as it had before their small confrontation on the racetrack. The man wasn't ever going to win any personality awards, that was for sure, but she felt a grudging respect for him.

Sambo purred and stretched his furry legs, his claws digging deep into the thick robe. Catherine stroked her pet, letting the long black tail slip through her fingers as she continued to mull over the time she and Royce had shared the track. The realization that she actually enjoyed their silent battle of wills warmed her from the inside out. For some unknown reason, she'd managed to amuse him. Because of the dark, Catherine hadn't been able to witness his stern features relax into a smile. She would have liked to have seen that, taken a picture to remind her that the man *could* smile.

Her stomach growled, and Catherine briefly wondered what was stashed in her freezer. Hopefully something would magically appear that she could toss in the microwave. She definitely wasn't in the mood to cook.

On her way into the kitchen, she paused in front of the photograph that rested on the fireplace mantel. The man staring back at her had deep brown eyes that were alive with warmth, wit and character.

Catherine's eyes.

He was handsome, so handsome that she often stared at the picture, regretting the fact she had never been given the chance to know him. She'd been only three when her father had been shipped to Vietnam, five when he'd been listed as Missing in Action. Often she'd reached back as far as her memory would take her to snatch hold of something that would help her remember him, but each time she was left to deal with frustration and disappointment.

The man in the photo was young, far too

young to have his life snuffed out. No one would ever know how he'd died or even when. All Catherine's family had been told was that his Navy jet had gone down over a Vietcong infested jungle. They never were to know if he survived the crash or had been taken prisoner. Those, like so many other details of his life and death, had been left to her imagination.

Catherine's mother, a corporate attorney, had never remarried. Marilyn Fredrickson wasn't bitter, nor was she angry. She was far too practical to allow such negative emotions to taint her life.

Like a true Navy wife, she'd silently endured the long years of the cruel unknowns, refusing to be defeated by the helplessness of frustration. When her husband's remains had been returned to the States, she'd stood proud and strong as he was laid to rest with full military honors.

The only time Catherine could ever remember her mother weeping had been the day her father's casket had arrived at the airport. With a gentleness and a sweetness that impressed Catherine still, her mother had walked over to the flag-draped casket, rested her gloved hand at the head and brokenly whispered, "Welcome home, my love." Then she'd slumped to her knees and sobbed until she'd released a ten-year reservoir of submerged emotions.

Catherine had cried with her mother that day. But in death, as he had been in life, Andrew Warren Fredrickson remained a stranger.

In choosing to become a Navy attorney, Catherine had followed both her parents' footsteps. Being a part of the military had brought her as close as she was likely to get to understanding the man who had given her life.

Lulled by her thoughts, Catherine ran the tip of her finger along the top of the gold frame. "I wonder if you ever had to work with someone like Royce Nyland," she said softly.

She did that sometimes. Talked to the photograph as though she honestly expected her father to answer. She didn't, of course, but carrying on a one-sided conversation with the man in the picture eased the ache in her heart at never having known him.

Sambo meowed loudly, announcing it was well past dinnertime, and Catherine had best do something quickly. The black feline waited impatiently in front of his bowl while Catherine brought out the pouch of soft cat food.

"Enjoy," she muttered, wincing as she bent over to fill the food dish. Holding her hand at the small of her back, Catherine cautiously straightened. Her pride had cost her more than she'd first realized.

* * *

"But, Dad, I've just got to have that jacket," Kelly announced as she carried her dinner plate over to the sink. She rinsed it off and set it in the dishwasher, a chore that went above and beyond her normal duties. As far as Royce was concerned, she was going to have to do a whole lot more than stack a few dishes to change his mind.

"You have a very nice jacket now," he reminded her, standing to pour himself a cup of coffee. He supposed he should be grateful she'd chosen to overlook the fact he was forty minutes later than he'd told her he would be. After her initial protest she'd been suspiciously forgiving. Now he knew why.

"But my jacket's from last year and it's really old and the sleeve has a little tear in it and no one is wearing fluorescent green anymore. I'll be the laughingstock of the entire school if I wear that old thing."

"That 'old thing' as you put it, will do nicely. The subject is closed, Kelly Lynn." Royce was determined not to give in this time. He was walking a fine line with his daughter as it was, and loomed dangerously close to overindulging her. It was easy to do. She was a sweet child, unselfish and gentle. Actually it was something of a wonder that Kelly should turn out to be such a considerate child. The ten-year-old had been raised by a succession of babysitters. From the time she was only a few weeks old, Kelly had been lackadaisically palmed off on others.

Sandy had only agreed to have one child, and she'd done so reluctantly six years into their marriage. Her career as a fashion buyer had dominated her life, so much so that Royce doubted that his wife had possessed a single mothering instinct. When she'd been killed in a freak auto accident, Royce had grieved for her loss, but their relationship had been dead for several years.

If Kelly had been shortchanged in the mother department, Royce wasn't convinced she'd done much better with him as a father. Heaven knew Royce's reputation was that of a hard-nosed bastard. But he was fair and everyone knew it. He did the best he could, but often wondered if that was good enough. He loved Kelly and he wanted to do right by her.

"All the other girls in school have new jackets," she mumbled under her breath.

Royce ignored the comment and between sips of coffee placed the leftovers inside the refrigerator.

"I've already saved $6.53 from my allowance?" She made the statement into a question, seeking a response.

Royce returned the carton of milk to the shelf.

"Missy Gilbert said the jackets were going to be on sale at J. C. Penney and with next week's allowance I'd have almost one fourth of the total cost. I'm trying real hard on my arithmetic this year, you know."

"Good girl." The two of them had suffered through more than one go-round with fractions.

Kelly turned her big baby blues full force on him. "What about the jacket, Dad?"

Royce could feel himself giving in. This wasn't good. He should be a pillar of strength, a wall of granite. He'd already told her once the subject was closed. The jacket she had now was good enough. He remembered when they'd bought it last year. Royce had been appalled at the outrageous shade of putrid green, but Kelly had assured him it was perfect and she would wear it two or three years.

"Dad?" she asked ever so sweetly, the way she always did when she sensed he was weakening.

"I'll think about it."

"Thanks, Dad," she cried, rushing across the room and hugging his waist. "You're the greatest."

An odd sense of self-consciousness attacked Catherine when she went down to the track the following evening. As she suspected, Royce was there ahead of her, running laps, as were several other men.

Royce hadn't said more than a handful of words to her all day, which wasn't unusual. He was as polite and as cool as always. When he came into the office that morning, he'd glanced her way, and Catherine could have sworn he was looking straight through her. His hard blue eyes had passed over her without so much as a flicker of friendliness. If she were to take the time to analyze his look, she suspected it had been one of cool indifference. It wasn't that Catherine expected him to throw his arms around her and greet her like a long lost friend. On second thought, maybe that was the problem.

They'd shared something on that running track, a camaraderie, an understanding and appreciation for each other. Catherine didn't expect warm embraces, but she hadn't expected him to regard her so impersonally. Apparently she'd read more into their talk than he intended.

That was her first mistake, and Catherine feared she was ready to commit mistake number two.

Squaring her shoulders, she traipsed down the hillside to the running track. She was later this evening than she had been the night before. No thanks to Commander Nyland. For the past two hours she'd been reviewing files and charting progress as the substitute coordinator for the physical fitness program. Her eyes hurt, her shoulders ached and she was in no mood to lock horns with the executive officer, unless, of course, he started something first.

Catherine completed her warming-up exercises and joined the others circling the quarter-mile track. She needed to unwind, vent the frustration she felt over being assigned this extra duty, which was an imposition she didn't need. It seemed that the commander had seen fit to delegate CDO duty that Friday night to someone else. Lucky for that someone.

Her first lap was relaxed. Catherine liked to ease herself into running, starting off slow and gradually gaining her momentum, peaking at about the second mile and finishing off the third in a relaxed stride.

Royce passed her easily on the first go-round. Catherine fully expected that he would. Once again she was impressed with the power and strength she felt as he shot past her. His skin was tan and his muscles bronzed. It was as if he were a living, moving work of art, perfect, strong and male. Her heart raced much faster than it should. A rush of sensation so powerful it nearly knocked her off her feet took her by surprise. On the heels of that emotion came another, one more potent than the first. Anger. He zoomed past her again and it was all she could do to hold herself back from charging ahead.

On the third lap she couldn't help herself, and she let loose, running as though she were in the Olympic time trial and this was her one and only chance to make the team.

The sense of satisfaction she gained leaping past Royce was enough to make her forget how hard she was pushing herself to maintain this stride.

The feeling of triumph was short-lived, as she knew it would be. Royce stepped up his pace and quickly charged around her. Then he slowed down and waited for her steps to join his.

"Good evening, Lieutenant Commander," he greeted, cordially enough.

"Commander." She wasn't in any mood to wish him a pleasant anything. Once again he'd managed to irritate her. No man had evoked such heated feelings from her, whether they be reasonable or unreasonable. It was all because of Royce Nyland that she'd been the one poring over a carload of files late into the afternoon.

Royce increased his stride, and Catherine struggled to keep even with him. She had the feeling that he could have left her to eat his dust at any time, and was simply toying with her the way a cat enjoys playing with a cornered mouse.

None of that seemed to matter as she pushed herself harder than ever.

After a couple of laps, Catherine sensed his amusement. No doubt she and her damnable pride were a keen source of entertainment to the obstinate executive officer.

Somehow Catherine managed to keep up with Royce for three complete laps, but she knew she couldn't continue the killing pace any longer. It was either drop out now or collapse. Catherine chose the former.

When she pulled back, slowed her pace to a fast walk, Royce raced ahead, then he surprised her by turning around and coming back. He kept his arms and feet in motion as he matched her speed.

"You all right?"

"Just ducky." She barely managed to breathe evenly, and prayed a sufficient amount of sarcasm leaked through to convey her mood.

A crooked smile slanted his mouth, his look cool and mocking. "Do you have a problem, Lieutenant Commander?"

"Off the record?" she asked, without hesitating. A month of frustration could no longer be contained, and she was bursting to let him know exactly what she thought of him.

"By all means."

Catherine might be digging herself in deeper

than she dare, but her patience was shot. "Is there something about me that troubles you, Commander?" She didn't give him time to respond, but rushed ahead, "Because something's rotten in Denmark, and frankly, it isn't my problem.... It's yours."

"I don't treat you any differently than anyone else," Royce inserted smoothly.

"Like hell you don't," she shot back heatedly. Thankfully the others had left the track, which might or might not be a blessing.

"I don't see you assigning anyone else to stand duty four weeks straight. For some unknown reason you've chosen to destroy my weekends. I've spent eleven years in this man's Navy and I've never stood duty more than once a month. Until you were assigned my XO. Apparently you don't like me, Commander, and I demand to know why."

A nerve twitched in his lean, hard jaw. "On the contrary, I find your dedication to duty to be highly commendable."

Catherine didn't actually expect him to admit his dislike of her, but she wasn't willing to listen to his military rhetoric, either. "I suppose my dedication to duty is what made you decide to bless me with this plush job of coordinating the physical fitness program? Was that supposed to be a bonus for all the extra hours I put in on the

Miller case? If so, find another way to thank me, would you?" She was trying to talk and draw in deep breaths at the same time and doubted that Royce could make out more than a few words.

Royce stiffened. "Is that all?"

"Not quite." She was only beginning to gain her momentum. "Off the record, Commander, I think you're a real jerk."

When she finished, Catherine was overwhelmed with a feeling of release. She started to tremble, but she wasn't sure if the shaking could be attributed to the fact she'd pushed herself physically to the point of collapse or that she'd stood on a military compound and shouted insults at her executive officer at the top of her lungs.

His look was impossible to read. The feeling in the pit of her stomach was decidedly uncomfortable.

"Is that a fact?" he demanded.

"Yes." Her voice wobbled with uncertainty, sounding as though it were coming from the bottom of a well. She drew in a deep breath, knowing she'd stepped over the boundaries of what should and shouldn't be said to a superior officer. The blood that seemed to have been pounding in her ears like ringing church bells suddenly went silent.

With her hands knotted into tight fists at her

sides, she braced herself for the backlash. If she thought to clear the air, she was sadly mistaken. If she'd accomplished anything it was to sabotage her own career.

Royce didn't say anything for several moments, but the nerve in his jaw continued twitching. Then he nodded as though they'd casually been discussing the weather, turned and resumed running. Catherine was left standing alone to stare after him.

Catherine spent an uncomfortable night, tossing and turning and finally talking over her troubles with Sambo. To her way of thinking, Royce would either ignore her outburst or see to it that she was transferred to a Third World country. However he reacted, she would be getting exactly what she deserved. No one spoke to their XO the way she had. No one.

For hours she lay awake analyzing what had happened. After several soul-searching sessions, she still didn't know what had caused her to get loose enough to say the things she did.

The following morning, Royce was already at his desk, behind closed doors when she arrived. She glanced cautiously toward his office. If there was a merciful God, then Commander Nyland would be willing to forget and forgive her outburst from the day before. She would apologize, grovel if need be, but leaving matters as they were was clearly unacceptable.

"Morning," she said gingerly to Elaine Perkins. "How's the great white hunter today?" she asked, hoping her secretary had had a chance to judge Royce's mood.

"Same as usual," Elaine told her, sipping coffee from a thick ceramic mug. Her voice drawled with a thick southern accent. "He asked me to send you into his office when you arrived."

Catherine felt the starch go out of her knees. "He asked to see me?"

"You heard me right. What are you looking so worried about? You haven't done anything, have you?"

"Nothing," Catherine whispered in reply. Nothing except stick her head in a noose and sling the other end of the rope over the highest branch in the tree.

Squaring her shoulders in her best military form, she walked across the office and knocked politely on the commander's door. When she was ordered to enter the room, she did so with her eyes focused straight ahead.

"Good morning, Lieutenant Commander."

"Sir."

"Relax, Catherine." He leaned back in his chair, his chin resting on folded hands as though he were still weighing his decision.

Relax, he'd told her to relax, only Catherine hadn't figured out how she was supposed to be at ease when her career was on the line. She hadn't joined the Navy like so many other women with her head in the clouds, seeking adventure, travel and a paid education. She knew from the beginning about the rigorous routine, the political infighting and the fact she'd be dealing with world-class chauvinists.

Nevertheless she loved being part of the Navy. She'd worked hard, and her efforts had been rewarded. Now this.

"Since our recent discussion I've been having second thoughts," Royce said flatly.

Catherine swallowed against the heaviness in her throat. She doubted if she could have spoken if she tried.

"From everything I've read about you, you have an excellent record." He leaned forward and closed her file. "Effective immediately, I'm removing you as the substitute coordinator of the physical fitness program, and assigning Lieutenant Johnson the duty."

Catherine was sure she hadn't heard him correctly. Her eyes, which had been trained on the opposite wall, skirted to his. A breathless moment passed before she could speak, "You're removing me from the physical fitness program?"

She couldn't have been more surprised had he announced he was working for the KGB.

"That's what I just said."

Catherine blinked, not knowing what to say. "Thank you, sir," she finally managed.

"That will be all," he said, dismissing her.

She hesitated. She'd wanted to apologize for her outburst from the day before, but one look told her Royce wasn't interested in listening to her list her excuses.

As it was, her knees were knocking so badly that she walked over to her desk, slumped into the chair and held on to the edge as though it were a lifeline.

Catherine didn't see Royce for the remainder of the day, for which she was grateful. It gave her time to sort through her emotions, which were as confused and tangled as thin gold chains. She didn't know what to make of the executive commander. Every time she had him figured out, he'd do something more to confuse her. Complicating the matter even further were her muddled feelings toward him. He was by far the most virile man she'd ever met. She couldn't be in the same room with him and not experience that magnetism. Yet, she found herself intensely disliking him.

An early October drizzle moistened the air

when Catherine walked out to the parking lot later that same afternoon. Rain, rain and more rain.

It was already dark, and her calf muscles were so sore she'd decided to skip running at the track. At least that was the excuse she'd given herself. How much truth there was to her rationale was something she'd prefer not to question.

Her GEO Storm was parked in the far end of the lot, and Catherine walked briskly toward it, hunching her shoulders against the chilly air. She opened her door, gratefully climbed inside and turned the ignition. Nothing. She tried again with the same results. The battery was completely dead.

With her hands braced against the steering wheel, Catherine groaned. She knew as much about the internal workings of a car as she did about performing brain surgery. Her automobile was only a few months old; surely there wasn't anything wrong with the engine.

Climbing out, she decided to check under the hood. How much good that would do was highly debatable, especially in the dark. It took her several minutes to find the clasp that would release the lock. In the dim light from the street lamp, she couldn't see much of anything.

The only thing she could think to do was call a towing service. She was walking back to her building when a low black sports car rolled past her, then circled around.

"Problems?" It was Royce Nyland.

Catherine froze, her first instinct was to claim she had everything under control and send him on his way. Lie, fib, anything that would postpone another encounter. She hadn't had the time to filter through her emotions from the one earlier in the day. Royce Nyland flustered her, and clouded her judgment. She wanted to dislike him, categorize him and wrap him up in one neat package. But every time she'd attempted to gain perspective, he did something to alter her opinion of him. He brought out the worst in her and yet she'd never worked harder to impress an officer. Then it came to her with driving force. She was sexually attracted to Royce Nyland.

Attracted in a way that spelled trouble for them both. As long as she was under his command, anything romantic between them was strictly prohibited. The Navy didn't pull any punches when it came to emotional involvement between men and women, one a supervisor to the other. Not even a hint of impropriety would be tolerated.

For her sake as well as his, she must ignore the fact her heart raced every time she saw him. She had to ignore the way her eyes sought him out whenever he walked into the room. When they were on the track together, she had to disregard the strength and power that radiated from him like warmth from a roaring fire. Royce Nyland was as off-limits to her as a married man.

"Is that your car?" he asked, obviously impatient with her lack of response.

"Yes...it won't start."

"I'll take a look at it for you."

Before she could tell him she was about to call for a tow truck, he switched gears and drove over to where her Storm was parked with its hood raised. By the time she walked back, he was sitting in the driver's seat.

"It looks like you left your lights on this morning. The battery's dead."

"Oh...I must have." She wasn't usually this slow-witted. Running around the track with Royce was one thing, but standing in the far end of the parking lot in the shadows was another. Instinctively she backed away.

"I have a battery cable in my car. I'll give you a start." It took only a matter of minutes for him to arrange the clamps linking the cables between the batteries of the two cars. They worked together and within a matter of minutes, her engine was purring contentedly.

She climbed out of the car while Royce disconnected the cable. Although it wasn't all that cold, she rubbed her hands together several times.

"Thank you."

He nodded, tossed the cable into the trunk of his car and was prepared to leave when she stopped him.

"Royce."

She hadn't meant to say his name, it had slipped out naturally. Apologizing had never come easy to her, but she owed him one—for the heat of her anger, the unreasonableness of her attack. "I shouldn't have said what I did the other night. If there's any excuse, it's that I was tired and short-tempered. It won't happen again."

"It was off the record, Fredrickson, don't worry about it." His mouth slowly curved into a smile. Their eyes met, solidly, hungrily and God help her, Catherine felt herself step toward him.

"I'm worried." But it wasn't what she'd said or done that she was talking about and she knew they both knew it. His eyes continued to detain hers. She'd never seen eyes so dark. They told her things she'd only suspected. Things she didn't want to know and had no business knowing.

He was lonely. So was she.

He was alone. So was she.

So alone she lay in bed at night and ached.

The need to be touched and held and kissed sometimes filled her with desperation.

She sensed the same desperation in Royce. It was what had drawn them together; it was what was keeping them apart.

The seconds throbbed between them like a giant time clock. Neither moved. Catherine dared not breathe. She was one step from walking directly into his arms, one word from spilling out everything she was feeling. The tension between them was as threatening as a thundercloud in a sky of blue. As strong as a prize fighter.

It was Royce who moved first. Away from her. Catherine sighed, her relief was so great.

"There won't be any problems," he whispered, turned and walked away.

She knew he wasn't speaking about her car.

Catherine wished she could believe it, but something told her it was far from the truth.

Royce was shaking. His hands were actually trembling as he sat in his own driveway, composing himself before he walked inside the house. He'd come so close to kissing Catherine that even now the thought of her filling his arms was enough to produce an ache so powerful, so sharp, it took his breath away. Royce was a man who thrived on discipline. He prided himself on his self-control, and yet he'd come a hair's space from tossing away everything he knew was right. And for what reason? Catherine Fredrickson turned him on.

For three years, Royce had shut off the valve that controlled his carnal appetites. He didn't need love, didn't need tenderness or require a woman's touch. Those were base emotions, best ignored. And neglect them he had until he'd met Catherine.

From the moment she'd walked into his office, he'd been confronted with a surge of unexpected, and unwanted feelings. He hadn't recognized what he was dealing with in the beginning. Subconsciously he had, otherwise he would never have gone out of his way to ruin her weekends by assigning her duty four Friday nights running. It didn't take a psychiatrist's couch to figure that one. He'd been batting a thousand when her name was the first one that drifted into his mind when he learned a substitute coordinator was going to be needed for the physical fitness program.

In analyzing his deeds, Royce realized he was punishing Catherine. With just cause. The lieutenant commander was a constant thorn in his flesh, a reminder that he was a man with needs that refused to be denied any longer.

Unfortunately there was a good deal more

at stake than satisfying a deep physical hunger. Catherine was under his command, which put pressure on them both. She was strictly off limits. Neither of them could afford to indulge in this attraction. It would only end up hurting them both. Their careers would suffer, and they'd both worked too damn hard to screw it up now over a few undisciplined hormones.

Dragging a fresh breath through his lungs, Royce closed his eyes and tried to push the picture of Catherine from his mind. He'd seen the emotions tearing at her in the parking lot, witnessed the pride-filled way in which she'd tilted her chin. Damn but the woman was proud. She apologized, accepting all the blame herself, although heaven knew everything she'd said was right. In that moment, he never respected a woman more. For her honesty, for her directness, for the fact she was willing to deal with whatever it was between them, lay it on the ground and call it what it was.

In those few words, heavy with meaning, Catherine had told him something he'd long suspected. Lieutenant Commander Catherine Fredrickson was a woman of substance. One so rare, one so beautiful, he didn't know what the hell he was going to do to get her out of his mind.

All he knew was that he must succeed even if it meant requesting a transfer and uprooting Kelly from the only home she'd ever known.

Three

"Can we go to a movie, too?" Kelly asked, snapping her seat belt into place. They were on their way to the Kitsap Mall, where the all-important jacket was on sale. It was either buy his daughter the coat or ruin her life before the eyes of her peers. Royce couldn't remember clothes and shoes being so vital when he was in grade school, but the world was a hell of a lot different place when he was ten.

"Dad," Kelly pressed, "what about a movie?"

"Sure," he agreed easily enough. Why not? He'd been short-tempered all week, due mainly to the fact he was dealing with his feelings for Catherine. Kelly deserved a reward for putting up with his sour mood.

As for what was happening—or better said, what was *not* happening—between him and Catherine, Royce had rarely spent a more uncomfortable week. He couldn't walk into the office without being aware of her. Her presence was like a time bomb silently ticking in the corner of the room. Every now and again their eyes would meet and he'd be left to watch the emotions race across the landscape of her dark brown eyes. With everyone around them in the office, there hadn't been a problem. It was the evening run that tested his soul.

Every afternoon Royce told himself he wouldn't run. Every afternoon, like precision clockwork, he was at the track, waiting for Catherine to arrive. They ran together, without speaking, without sharing, without looking at each other.

It was uncanny the comfort he found circling the track with the petite lieutenant commander at his side. The track was neutral ground, safe territory for them both. Those all-too-short minutes with Catherine were the reason he got out of bed in the morning, the reason he made it through the day.

When she smiled at him, Royce swore her eyes scored his heart. In the evenings when they'd finished jogging, Catherine would thank him for the workout and then silently return to her car. The moment she was out of sight, Royce was left feeling bereft. He hadn't realized what poor company a disciplined life-style could make, and what poorer company the long, lonely nights in an empty bed could be. The desolation was as powerful as a blow to his gut.

The evenings were another matter. He almost feared sleep because the moment he slipped into unconsciousness, Catherine filled his mind. She was soft and warm, and so real that all he had to do was reach out and draw her to his side. Royce would never have guessed his mind would play such cruel tricks on him. He was having trouble enough keeping Catherine at a distance, emotionally and physically. In sleep, his mind welcomed her, tormenting him with dreams he couldn't control. Dreams of Catherine running toward him on the beach, holding her arms out to him. Catherine feminine and soft in his embrace. Catherine laughing. Royce swore he never heard a sound more beautiful in all his life.

If there was anything to be grateful for, and it was damn little, it was the fact the dreams had never developed into anything even remotely physical between them.

In the mornings, Royce woke annoyed with himself, annoyed at Catherine for refusing to leave him alone and irritated with the world. With all the strength of his will, which was admittedly formidable, Royce pushed all thoughts of the lieutenant commander from his mind.

For as long as Catherine was under his command, all Royce could indulge himself in were involuntary dreams. He refused to allow himself the pleasure of recapturing the fantasy of him and Catherine alone together in quiet moments. Unhurried moments. With no demands. No deadlines. Moments when his heart and his soul were at rest.

Life could be a cruel hoax, Royce sharply reminded himself. He'd been taught that time and time again. He wasn't about to lose everything that was important to him over a woman, even if she did have eyes that looked straight through him.

The mall was crowded, but then it generally was on weekends, especially now that folks were gearing up for Christmas. Royce allowed Kelly to drag him into the J. C. Penney store. But that was only the beginning of the ordeal. The jacket she was so keen on had sold out in her size. The helpful salesclerk had phoned three other stores and there wasn't a single one available. Even the catalog had sold out.

"I'm sorry, sweetheart," Royce told her. She was bitterly disappointed and trying hard not to show it.

"Do you want to look around for a different coat?" Surely there was a father-of-the-year award for him in this offer. They'd spent nearly an hour on this wild-goose chase already, and Royce's patience had worn paper thin.

Kelly sat on the wooden bench outside the department store, her head bent low. Royce was about to repeat the question when she shrugged.

"How about something to drink?" Royce was half an hour overdue for a cup of coffee.

Kelly nodded eagerly. She stood and slipped her small hand into his. She didn't do that often, and Royce guessed she did so now needing his reassurance.

Royce bought her a Pepsi and himself a cup of fresh, hot coffee while Kelly scouted out a place for them to sit. Since it was close to noon, the tables were mostly occupied. They found one and sat down in the white wire chairs.

"Dad," Kelly whispered excitedly, "look at that pretty lady over there."

Hell, as far as Royce could see, the entire mall was filled with pretty ladies. "Where?"

"The one in the pink-and-green-and-blue jacket. Over there." Knowing it was impolite to point, Kelly wiggled her index finger back and forth in the general direction of where she wanted him to look. "Look, she's sorta walking toward us. Hurry and look before she turns away."

As he'd mused earlier, life could be filled with cruel hoaxes, and it was about to play another one on him now. Before he even realized what he was doing, Royce was on his feet. "Hello, Catherine."

"Royce." Her dark eyes were bright with surprise as well, and frankly, she didn't look any more pleased than he felt.

"How are you?" he heard himself ask stiffly.

"Fine."

"Dad." Impatiently, Kelly tugged on the hem of his leather jacket. "I like her coat...a whole lot."

Royce watched as Catherine's eyes momentarily left his and landed on Kelly. Once again surprise registered in the dark depths, but was quickly replaced by a gentleness and warmth that tightened strong cords around his heart. He'd never mentioned his daughter, and it was apparent she hadn't known he'd been married. Maybe she thought he was married still.

"This is my daughter, Kelly," Royce said, his voice low and throaty.

"Hello, Kelly. I'm Catherine." She dragged her eyes away from him and held out her hand to his daughter. "Your dad and I work together." She said this, Royce was convinced, as a reminder to them both. Hell, he didn't need it.

"Your jacket is real pretty," Kelly said quietly. She continued to tug on Royce's sleeve until he was convinced she'd pulled the armhole down to his elbow.

"What Kelly would like to know is where you bought it," Royce inserted dryly.

"And if they have kid sizes?" the ten-year-old asked excitedly.

"I got it right here in the mall, in Jacobson's."

"Dad," Kelly said, pushing aside her drink, "let's go look, okay?"

Royce glanced longingly at his coffee. He'd barely had time to take a single sip. Kelly was looking at him as if to say Jacobson's was sure to sell out in the next ten minutes if they didn't get there.

"I don't know if they have kid sizes," Kelly stated urgently, as though another five or ten minutes was sure to make the difference. "I know it's a ladies' store and everything, but you can wait outside if you want and I'll go in by myself."

"Why don't I take you down," Catherine suggested.

It took a fair amount of self-control not to leap up and kiss her. "You don't mind?" He had to ask. Pride demanded that much, at least.

"Not a bit. Go ahead and enjoy your coffee," Catherine suggested, her gaze returning to him. "We won't be more than a few minutes."

He should refuse. Royce knew it the minute

she made the offer, but Kelly was looking up at him, her eyes alive with excitement, and before he could argue with himself, he nodded.

A daughter, Catherine mused. Royce had a daughter. Catherine had worked with him for five weeks, and no one had bothered to mention the fact he'd been married or that he was raising Kelly. The child was incredibly sweet, with long dark hair and eyes so blue they reminded Catherine of wild bluebonnets. Kelly was as gentle and cute as Royce was remote and indifferent.

Catherine had noted how closely Royce had watched her when he introduced Kelly. His eyes had darkened into a brittle defiance as though he expected her to do or say something about the fact she hadn't known about the child. She found herself staring at him and the proud lines of his chiseled features. Catherine's gaze had moved smoothly from father to daughter. There was no doubt in her mind the two were related. Kelly possessed the same beautiful blue eyes, and although her face was heart-shaped and feminine, she was clearly a Nyland.

Until she'd walked into the shopping complex, Catherine hadn't realized how hungry she was for the sight of Royce. From clear across the other side of the mall, she'd walked directly to his side, guided by instinct to the man who'd dominated her thoughts for days on end.

"We went to the J. C. Penney store," Kelly explained as they walked side by side down the wide concourse, "but all the jackets in my size were sold. We looked and looked and I was feeling really low so Dad bought me a Pepsi and then we saw you," Kelly explained in one giant breath. "Your jacket is just perfect."

Catherine had bought it a couple of weeks earlier. Being new to the Pacific Northwest, she needed something heavier than a raincoat. The jacket had caught her eye in a ski shop, and although Catherine didn't ski, she'd been attracted to the colors, just the way Kelly had.

"I like it, too. And as I recall, they did have children's sizes."

"Dad doesn't like to shop much," Kelly explained as they wove their way between the moving crowd. "He does it for me, but I know he'd rather be watching a silly football game. Men are like that, you know?"

"So I've heard." As far as understanding the male of the species, Royce's daughter knew a whole lot more than Catherine did. For as long as she could remember, it had always been her and her mother. In college she'd lived in a girls' dormitory.

"Dad tries real hard, but he doesn't understand a lot of things about girls."

Catherine couldn't help grinning at that. Evidently she wasn't the only one at a loss when it came to understanding the opposite sex. Apparently what she and Royce needed was a ten-year-old to straighten out their lives.

They found the store, and indeed there was a jacket almost identical to the one Catherine had that was in Kelly's size. After Royce's daughter tried it on and modeled it in front of a mirror, Catherine had the salesclerk put it on hold.

Kelly raced back to the large open eating area to tell Royce about the rare find. Catherine followed close behind.

"It's got pink and green and blue. Not the same shade of blue as Catherine's, but almost. I can have it, can't I?" She dug into her small pocket at the top of her jeans and dragged out the five single dollar bills one at a time and then several coins from a different pocket. "I'll pay for part of it."

Royce stood and tossed the empty coffee cup into the garbage. "All right, all right. I know when I'm defeated." He glanced over at Catherine and winked.

Catherine couldn't believe it. The iceman winked as if he were a regular human being. Royce Nyland was one man in the office, another on the running track and someone else entirely different when he was with his daughter.

"I…can see you've got everything under control here," Catherine said, thinking she should probably leave. She felt awkward with Royce.

"Don't go," Kelly cried, reaching for Catherine's hand with both of her own. "Dad said he'd buy me pizza for lunch, and I want you to come, too."

"I'm sure Catherine has other plans," Royce said matter-of-factly.

Catherine noted that he didn't repeat the invitation, which was just as well. Yet, she couldn't hold back the sense of disappointment. "Yes, I do have some things to do. I was just going into the pet store to buy my cat a new litter box."

"I love the pet store," Kelly piped in eagerly. "Once they even let me hold a new puppy. I wanted to buy it real bad, but Dad said we couldn't because there wouldn't be anyone home during the day to take care of him."

Catherine's heart melted as she gazed down on Royce's daughter. So young and tender. Catherine remembered herself at that age and how life had been such a wonderful adventure then.

"Oh, do come, Catherine. Please."

Catherine's gaze moved to Royce. She expected his eyes to be cool and unreadable as they were so much of the time. Instead she found them troubled and unsure, yet inviting. Catherine felt as if the air had been sucked from her lungs.

"I...are you sure I wouldn't be intruding?" By everything that was right, she knew she should refuse. They were standing so close to the fire, close enough to get burned, and yet they each seemed to be taking turns tossing kindling into the flames.

"I'm sure," Royce answered.

"Oh, good," Kelly cried, seemingly unaware of the tension between Catherine and her father. "I certainly hope you don't like anchovies. Dad gets them on his half whenever we order pizza. Those things are disgusting."

A half hour later, they were sitting in a pizza parlor. Catherine and Kelly shared an Italian sausage and olive pizza pie while Royce ate his own, covered with the tiny fish both women found so offensive.

Although it was comfortably warm inside the restaurant, Kelly insisted upon wearing her new coat.

"Are those fingernails actually yours?" Kelly asked halfway through the meal.

Catherine nodded, her mouth full of pizza.

"You mean you don't have a single acrylic tip?"

It was incredible to Catherine that a ten-year-old knew about such things. "Not even one," she assured the girl.

Kelly's eyes widened with renewed respect. She held up her hand for Catherine to examine, showing the short, stubby ends of her own nails. Catherine reached for her purse and brought out her fingernail kit for Kelly to examine, explaining each instrument.

"What are you two talking about?" Royce demanded in mock exasperation. "As near as I can figure, you women have your own language."

Kelly reverently closed the case and returned it to Catherine. Her eyes drifted from Royce to her and then back again. Catherine could almost see the tiny wheels churning in the little girl's head.

"Are you married, Catherine?" The girl asked innocently enough.

"Ah...no." Catherine's throat felt tight and dry all of a sudden.

"Neither is my dad," the ten-year-old added, her words fraught with meaning. "My mom died, you know?" Kelly said it with complete lack of emotion, as though losing a mother was simply part of growing up.

"No...I wasn't aware of that." Catherine avoided looking at Royce.

Kelly took another couple of moments to assess the situation. "So you and my dad work together?"

"Kelly Lynn." Royce used a tone Catherine had heard often in the office. It brought trained sailors to attention, and it worked just as well with his daughter.

"I was only asking."

"Then don't."

"All right, all right, but I didn't mean anything by it." Royce's daughter returned to her pizza, took a bite and chewed two or three times before adding. "Catherine's coming to the movie with us, isn't she?" The question was directed to Royce, who once more narrowed his eyes at his daughter.

"I'll let you choose the movie if you want," Kelly offered. Evidently the choice of which film they'd see was a long-standing battle between them, and that she'd offer to let him pick was a major concession.

Catherine didn't know what Royce was waiting for. He shouldn't even be entertaining his daughter's suggestion. The fact they were having lunch together was one thing, but sitting in a movie theater together would be...should be out of the question.

"Dad?" Kelly probed.

Royce looked to Catherine, and his hard blue eyes held hers for the long, drawn-out moment.

Tension thickened the air until she was convinced neither of them was breathing.

"Catherine has other things to do," Royce informed his daughter.

Catherine was quick to reassure Kelly. "I really do, sweetheart. Perhaps we can all go another time."

Royce's young daughter accepted Catherine's decision with a quick nod, but it was apparent the girl was disappointed. She wasn't the only one. Catherine's heart felt as heavy as concrete. She'd never felt closer to Royce than this time with his daughter. He'd lowered his guard enough for her to glimpse the nurturing, caring man shielded behind the thick wall of pride and tradition.

After wiping her hands clean with a napkin, Catherine reached for her purse and slid from the booth. "Thank you both for lunch, but I really should be going."

Kelly slid out of the booth, too. "I wish you were going to the movie with us."

Her eyes found Royce's as she whispered, "So do I."

Catherine was halfway to the door when Royce stopped her. For a moment he didn't say anything, but stared down at her. His face revealed none of his thoughts, and briefly Catherine was aware of what a talent he possessed to hide his emotions so well.

His eyes continued to hold hers and seemed to scorch her with their intensity before he spoke, listing the movie and the time. "In case you change your mind," he said, before turning back to his daughter.

By the time Catherine was inside her car, she'd started to tremble. What was the matter with Royce? Had he gone mad? Had she?

Royce, her XO, knowing what they were both risking, seemed to be telling her he wanted her to come to the movie. But he was leaving the decision in her hands. God help them both, she wanted it, too.

A movie wasn't an affair, she reminded herself. If they both happened to show up at the same movie at the same time, no one would put the wrong connotation on that. The rule book didn't say they couldn't be friends. If friends just happened to meet at a movie, it wouldn't be unheard of for them to sit together. Would it?

Catherine didn't know what to do. Her head was telling her one thing, and her heart another. Both their careers could be jeopardized. It was far too much to risk for the pleasure of sitting next to each other in a matinee.

Yet when the time approached, Catherine was behind a line of preteens. Her heart was hammering so loudly, she was convinced everyone around her must be able to hear it, too. Once she glanced over her shoulder, thinking the shore patrol was on her tail. The thought was ludicrous, which only went to prove the state of her mind.

Royce was sitting in the last row, with Kelly in the seat next to him. The girl noticed Catherine immediately and leaped up from her chair as though she'd been sitting on a giant coiled spring. She hurriedly scooted down the aisle and enthusiastically hugged Catherine.

"I was hoping you'd come." She grabbed Catherine's hand and energetically led her to the seats.

Catherine didn't look at Royce. She feared what she'd read in his eyes.

"Missy's here," Kelly cried, and waved madly, as though the fate of the free world depended on how quickly her friend recognized her. "Can I go show her my new coat?"

Royce's hesitation was noticeable before he agreed, and Kelly raced away.

Catherine sat down, leaving an empty seat between them

Royce continued to look straight ahead as though he'd never seen her in his life. "Are you crazy?" he hissed under his breath after an exaggerated moment. But it was the kind of anger that comes from caring too much, directed at himself as much as at her.

"Are you?" she came back just as heatedly. She was equally furious and for all the same reasons. She wasn't going to take the blame for this. She'd made her decision and her excuses at the restaurant. They both had. He was the one who'd dropped the anchor in her lap by making a point of letting her know which movie and what showing. He'd blatantly asked her to come, and now he seemed to regret she was there.

"Yes, I think I am crazy," Royce admitted reluctantly.

"I wasn't going to come," she told him softly. Even after he'd let it be known he wanted her with him and Kelly.

"Then why did you?"

Catherine didn't know. Maybe it was because she liked to live dangerously, walk as close to the edge of the cliff as possible without falling off. "I don't know. Why did you?"

Royce chuckled, but there was no amusement in his laugh. "Hell, I don't know. I guess I like tampering with the fates."

"Dad." Kelly was scooting down the narrow row sideways in a rush to return to her father. "Missy wants me to sit with her. You don't care, do you?"

Once again Royce hesitated before answering. "Go ahead."

"Thanks, Dad." Kelly scooted past Catherine, paused and winked. Winked! The same way Royce had winked at her earlier. Only she didn't know what Kelly meant any more than she'd understood the gesture from Royce.

Kelly left to join her friend, and the tension between her and Royce was so strong, Catherine didn't know if she could endure it any longer.

"I'll move." She started to stand, when he stopped her.

"No," Royce said automatically, his hand grasping her arm. "Stay." The word was soft and pleading.

Catherine couldn't refuse him, and when she sat down, he moved one seat over, sitting next to her. Almost immediately the theater darkened and music filled the room. Royce stretched out his long legs, and his thigh inadvertently brushed hers. Catherine's breath caught in her throat at the sudden rush of sensation that raced up and down her limb. Royce, too, gave a small gasp. The firm pressure of his leg felt muscular and hard. It was funny how easy it was for her to forget how good a man can feel. Catherine glanced up to find Royce openly studying her. His eyes were bright with a heat that warmed her from the top of her head to the soles of her feet. With a determined effort she dragged her gaze away from his.

Royce shifted his weight and with a good deal of reluctance moved his leg. They both breathed a little easier. This was difficult enough without adding more temptation, more fuel to the fire.

Catherine doubted that either one of them was able to follow the plot of the movie. If anyone had asked her, Catherine wouldn't have been able to discuss a single detail. Her concentration was centered on the man sitting next to her.

At some point, Royce thrust a bucket of popcorn between them. In an effort to fix her attention on the screen, Catherine reached for a handful of the kernels and ate them one by one. About the third or fourth dip into the bucket, Catherine's hand inadvertently bumped Royce's. She quickly withdrew her fingers, only Royce wouldn't allow it. He reached out and grasped her hand, then slowly, as if damning himself for his weakness, laced his fingers one by one with hers. His grip was tight, his nails cutting into her smooth flesh. It was as though he never intended on letting her go. The bucket of popcorn disappeared, and still Royce held her hand.

There was no way Catherine could explain the tumult of emotion that overtook her at the gesture. A host of unexplainable sensations assailed her, hidden, unrecognized emotions were

so prominent that her head started to spin. If he
was kissing her or touching her breasts or making love to her, Catherine could have understood, could have accepted her reaction.

But all he was dong was holding her hand.

She'd never felt more vulnerable or more ex-
posed. She was risking everything that was important to her. Royce was taking a chance with
his career, and for what?

The question was a harsh one, and the answer…the answer was even harsher. She knew
next to nothing about Royce. He'd been married, his wife had died and there was a child.
He was Navy, a man born to lead others. He
was respected. Admired. But they'd never sat
down and talked about their lives, never shared
anything beyond the basic everyday-working-
together kind of conversation. That they should
experience this powerful pull toward each other,
this forceful attraction, was a quirk of nature.
There was no rhyme. No reason. Yet it would
have taken an act of congress to move Catherine
out of that movie theater.

The film ended. Catherine was hardly aware
of the fact until he released her hand. She
wanted to protest, longing to maintain the contact, as innocent as it was, until the last possible moment.

"Catherine," he whispered, leaning close. "Go now."

"But…"

"For the love of God, don't argue with me. Just leave."

Something in his voice, a warning, a threat, Catherine didn't know which, prompted her to move quickly. "I'll see you Monday," she said, standing.

But she'd be thinking about him every minute in between.

"Is there something going on between you and Commander Nyland?" Elaine Perkins asked Monday morning when Catherine arrived for work.

Her heart sank to her knees before quickly rebounding. "What makes you ask that?" she asked, forcing her voice to remain light and breezy.

"He wants to see you first thing. Again."

"He wants to see me first thing?" Catherine was beginning to sound like an echo.

"And when the almighty commander speaks, we obey," Elaine said as a means of reminding them both. "All I want to know is what you've done this time?"

"What makes you think I did anything?" Catherine asked as she hung up her coat.

"Because he looks like he's in a mood to wrestle crocodiles. That man is as mean as a shark with a toothache, and if I were you, I wouldn't tangle with him."

"Don't worry." Squaring her shoulders, she approached Royce's office and knocked politely.

"Come in." His frown deepened when he saw her. Perkins was right; Royce didn't look any too cheerful. The iceman had returned. Gone was the indulgent father, replaced by the man so ingrained in military procedure Catherine was convinced she had been imagining someone else on Saturday.

"Sit down, Lieutenant Commander." She wasn't Catherine any longer, but a rank.

She did as he requested, not knowing what to expect.

Royce rolled a pencil between his palms. "I don't think it's a good idea for us to continue exercising together in the afternoons."

Catherine's eyes flew to his. It was the only thing they shared, that time together, and although it was entirely selfish of her, she didn't want to give it up.

"I realize you have as much right to use the track as I do, so I'd like to suggest a schedule. Unfortunately the afternoons are the only time I'm free...."

"My schedule if far less restrictive, *sir*," she

said, bolting to her feet. "Don't worry. I'll make an effort to avoid any possibility of us meeting. Would you like me to stop frequenting the Kitsap Mall while I'm at it?"

The telltale muscle leaped in his jaw. Catherine didn't know why she was taking the offensive so strongly. He was only saying and doing what needed to be done, what should have been said long before now. But she felt as if the rug had been pulled from beneath her feet and she was teetering for her balance.

"You may shop wherever you choose."

"Thank you," she returned crisply. "Is that all?"

"Yes."

Catherine turned to leave.

"Catherine…" He stopped her as she reached his door. She turned back, but he shook his head. "Nothing, you may go."

Four

Catherine understood. Conclusively. Decisively.

Commander Royce Nyland, her executive officer, she reminded herself, was shutting her out. Apparently it was easy enough to do. He'd rerouted his emotions so often that barricading any and all feelings for her was a simple matter.

She, unfortunately, wasn't achieving the same level of success. Royce Nyland had invaded her life. As hard as she tried, her efforts to adjust her own attitude had done little, if any, good.

She didn't want to feel the things she did for him, and frankly she didn't know how to deal with them. This was a new experience for her. How was she supposed to block him from her mind when thoughts of him filled every minute of every day?

He'd ordered her to stop, she reminded herself. When a superior officer spoke, Catherine, ever loyal, ever Navy, obeyed. No one had told her it was going to be easy. But then again, no one had bothered to explain how damn difficult it would be, either.

Nothing like this had ever happened to Catherine before, and frankly... Frankly, she didn't want it happening to her now.

Royce didn't want to jeopardize his career. She didn't want to jeopardize hers, either. He had little use for love in his life; she'd lived without it so long she didn't know what she was missing. If he could ignore the empty hole that grew deeper and wider with each passing day, then, she determined, so could she.

Maintaining her daily exercise program became of primary importance to Catherine. Never having liked running in the streets, she ran on the base track at odd hours of the day. She was careful not to infringe on Royce's time, holding on to this small link with him because it was all she had.

Early Friday morning, two weeks after Royce had called her into his office for their latest discussion, Catherine parked her car close to the jogging track.

She'd just finished her second lap when another runner joined her, coming up from behind her, gaining on her easily.

"Good morning."

Catherine's throat constricted. She'd worked

so hard not to intrude on his exercise time, running in the early morning hours in order to avoid the possibility of them stumbling into each other.

The immediate sense of unfairness and out-rage was nearly overwhelming. Instantly she wanted to confront Royce, shout at him, de-mand that he leave her alone, but he spoke first. "You're angry."

"You're damn right I am. What are you doing here?" Her voice was low and accusing. Sud-denly she felt tired. Tired of pretending. Tired of ignoring emotions so strong she was chok-ing on them. Tired of hiding.

"I need to talk to you."

"So talk." Her nerves were raw, stretched to the breaking point. They had been for weeks.

They jogged half a lap before he spoke. For someone who was so eager to communicate, for someone who'd broken the very rules he'd initiated, he seemed to be having a hard time getting started.

"I had to do it, Catherine," he said with enough force to shake the ground. The words weren't loud, but packed with emotion. "We've both been in the Navy too long, and love it too much to risk everything now."

"I know." Her anger vanished as quickly as it had risen and her voice trembled slightly despite her best efforts to keep it even and unaffected. She wasn't nearly as good as Royce when it came to disguising her emotions.

"What I didn't realize was how damn difficult it was going to be." He said this softly, as though admitting to a wrongdoing, as though it were important she know.

Catherine knotted her hands tightly at her sides. She never expected him to admit it, never dreamed he would. He'd given every indication that pushing her from his thoughts, from his heart, hadn't caused him a moment's concern. Surely he must have known how difficult it was for her. She'd buried herself in her work, repainted her entire apartment, stayed up late listening to Johnny Mathis records in a futile effort to forget Royce. But nothing worked. Nothing.

"Kelly asks about you every night," Royce confessed next.

"I'm sorry," she whispered, knowing that involving his daughter in this had made everything more difficult. "I didn't purposely run into you that day."

"I know. I'm not blaming you, I just wish to hell it hadn't happened. No," he altered quickly, regretfully, "that isn't true. I'm thankful Kelly met you."

"It would have been better for us both if it

hadn't happened." Yet Catherine would always be grateful for that one day with Royce and his daughter. It gave her something to hold on to for all the long, lonely nights.

"There's a rumor going around," Royce said after a moment. Catherine's heart tripped. The fear must have shown in her eyes because Royce added, "It's not about us, don't worry."

The military abounded with rumors. That Royce thought it important enough to repeat one to her meant something was deeply troubling him.

"I heard by means of the grapevine that I may be sent over to Turkey to work at NATO."

His words fell like heavy stones upon Catherine's heart, each one inflicting a sharper, more profound pain. "Oh, Royce." Her tone was low and hesitant, filled with concern.

"If I am, I'll need someone to take Kelly for me."

Catherine would do it in a heartbeat, but surely there was someone else. A relative or a long-standing family friend. As a single parent, Royce must have completed a parenting plan so there would be someone to take Kelly with as little as twenty-four-hours' notice.

"I spoke to Kelly about the possibility of us being separated last night. I didn't want to alarm her, but at the same time I didn't think it was fair to hide it from her, either."

Catherine nodded, impressed with his wisdom in dealing honestly with his daughter.

"Kelly's lived in Bangor all her life, and I'd hate to uproot her."

"I understand." The ten-year-old had already lost her mother, and if her father were to be given shipping orders to the Middle East, everything that was familiar to Kelly would be stripped from her. The fact he'd been stationed at Bangor this long was something of an oddity.

"Sandy's family lives in the Midwest. She was never close to her mother and had lost contact with her father several years before. She has a couple of stepbrothers, but I've never bothered to keep in touch with them. To be honest, I haven't heard from her side of the family since the funeral."

"Kelly can stay with me," Catherine offered.

They had stopped running by this time and were walking the track, their pace invigorating. The air was cold and clean, and when Royce spoke, his breath created a thin fog in the autumn morning.

"If you can't, my parents will be happy to have her, but they're living in a retirement community in Arizona, and frankly, I hate to complicate their lives at this point."

"I mean it, Royce. I'd love to have Kelly stay with me."

"Thank you," he whispered. His voice was hoarse, and intuitively Catherine knew how difficult it was for Royce Nyland to admit he needed someone for something. Knowing he needed her, even if it was for his daughter's sake, did something to her heart. Her vulnerable heart. Susceptible only to him.

Royce picked up the pace, and they resumed jogging at a leisurely pace.

"How's Kelly taking the news?" Catherine asked, concerned about the grade schooler.

"Like a real trooper. I think she's more excited about the possibility of living with you, something she suggested by the way, than she's concerned about me leaving."

"Typical kid reaction."

"She really took to you."

Catherine smiled, her heart warming. "I took to her, too."

Royce laughed. It was the first time Catherine could remember ever hearing Royce amused.

"What's so funny?"

Royce sobered almost immediately. "Something Kelly said. Hell, I didn't even know she wanted a sister."

"A sister?"

Royce looked away abruptly. "Never mind," he said curtly.

They circled the track once more, their time slipping away like sand between splayed fingers. It felt so good to be with Royce, these moments together were like a rare, unexpected gift meant to be savored and enjoyed. Catherine had trouble keeping her eyes off him. He was tall and lean, his muscular shoulders broad. The sunlight was breaking over the hill, glinting on his thick, dark hair.

They parted at the last possible minute. Royce left first, heading toward the office. Catherine took a hurried shower. She stood under the spray, letting it pelt against her face and tried not to think of Royce being transferred all the way to Turkey.

It would solve one problem; she wouldn't be under Royce's command and if they chose to become romantically involved the Navy would not care. Of course they'd be separated by thousands of miles, but the Navy generally went out of its way to make falling in love difficult.

Catherine arrived at the office, feeling refreshed. She greeted her secretary, poured herself a cup of coffee and sat down at her desk. She didn't look for Royce, but lately she'd made a habit of not seeking him out, even if it was only with her eyes.

She was absorbed in her own work for an hour or more when Commander Parker strolled into her office. Catherine had briefly met Commander Parker when she was first assigned to the Bangor station. He was in his mid-thirties, single and something of a flirt. He'd asked Catherine out to dinner one of the Friday nights Royce had seen fit to assign her duty, and she'd been forced to refuse. Apparently he'd taken her rejection personally, and hadn't asked her out since.

"Have you seen Commander Nyland?" Elaine Perkins asked a minute or so later.

"He was on the track this morning," Catherine explained as nonchalantly as she could. "He left before I did and I haven't seen him since."

"Commander Parker's looking for him."

"I'm sorry, I can't help."

Perkins left and returned a few minutes later after a flurry of activity from several others. Apparently Royce wasn't anywhere to be found, which was highly uncommon. Catherine worked hard at disguising her growing concern.

The phone rang; Elaine Perkins answered, routing the call. Her hand was still on the receiver when she turned to Catherine. "I didn't know Commander Nyland had a daughter.

Somehow I can't picture old stoneface as a parent."

Catherine grinned. Not long ago she would have thought the same thing herself. But she'd seen Royce interact with his daughter, seen the love and pride shining through his eyes as he looked down at her. "She's ten and an absolute delight," Catherine said before she could stop herself.

"So you've met her?"

"Ah…I ran into them at the mall a couple of weeks back," Catherine explained, returning her attention to the case she was reviewing.

"If you've met her," Elaine continued, emotion bleeding into her voice, "then you might be interested in knowing where Commander Nyland disappeared to. Apparently his daughter was hit by a car on her way to school. She's at the Navy Hospital."

Catherine swore her heart stopped in that moment. She went stiff with shock, then completely numb. Slowly she rose to her feet and blindly looked around her as if the air circulating the room would tell her it wasn't so.

Oh my God. Oh my God. Not Kelly. Please not Kelly, Catherine's mind chanted. The phrase kept repeating itself in her mind, a prayer, an entreaty to the heavenly powers to watch over the child Royce loved so dearly.

"Catherine?" She couldn't look at Elaine, fearing she would read the stark terror in her eyes and know how much Royce and his daughter meant to her.

"Did…what's her condition?"

"I don't know. Are you all right?"

"I'm fine," she answered, reaching for her purse. "I'm…I'm taking my lunch hour."

"Sure thing," Elaine returned hesitantly. "I don't suppose you noticed it's only ten. It's a little early for lunch, don't you think?"

Catherine didn't bother to answer. She was already on her way out of the office. She rushed down the stairs and shot out of the building. It amazed her how calm she was. Outwardly, she was as cool and composed as an admiral. On the inside she was quaking with fear so stark and real the taste of it filled her mouth.

Please God, not Kelly. She must have repeated the phrase a hundred times as she raced across the asphalt parking lot to her car.

Catherine didn't remember any part of the fifteen-minute drive to the Navy Hospital in Bremerton. One moment she was at the Navy Base at Bangor, and the next thing she knew she was pulling into the hospital parking lot.

The emergency room receptionist must have recognized the urgency in Catherine's eyes, and after a few preliminary questions, directed her to the third floor.

She took the elevator up, repeating the room number over and over in her head as she raced down the wide polished corridor. The door was ajar when Catherine arrived.

Kelly, her face ashen against the sheets, was either asleep or unconscious, the metal railing around the bed raised. Catherine's heart, which had only recently righted itself, tripped into double time. Once more she prayed for the little girl who had come to mean so much to her in so short a time. Tears filled her eyes, and she bit into her lower lip in an effort to keep them at bay.

Royce was sitting in a chair next to the hospital bed, his face in his hands, oblivious to her presence.

"Royce."

He lifted his head, turned and fixed his eyes on her. He frowned as though he didn't believe it was her, as though he desperately needed an anchor. His face was ravaged with emotion, scored with myriad fears. Briefly he closed his eyes before he stood and walked over to her.

Thankfully Catherine had the presence of mind to close the door. No sooner had it swung shut when Royce hauled her to him, lifted her from the floor and locked his arms around her waist. A shudder ran down the length of him as he breathed in deeply and buried his face in the gentle slope of her shoulder.

Catherine felt the moisture slide down her cheeks, and she held on to Royce with equal ferocity, her arms looped around his neck.

"She's going to be all right," Royce assured her several moments later, his words more breath than sound. As if he feared he was hurting her, he relaxed his hold and slowly, hesitantly lowered her feet to the ground. "She's asleep now. The doctor wanted to keep her overnight for observation. Oh God, Catherine, it was so close, so very close. A few more feet and I might have lost her."

His eyes continued to hold hers. The barriers were down now, and she understood so many things he'd never allowed her to see before. Though he wished she'd never been transferred from Hawaii. Though he wished she was in anyone else's command but his. Though he wished to hell she'd stayed outside his life. He needed her. He needed her because he couldn't endure seeing his only child hurt and stand at her bedside alone. He needed her then. He needed her tomorrow. The need wasn't ever going to go away.

Without thinking, Catherine did what seemed natural. She reached up and pressed her head to his chest, reassuring him the only way she knew how. His hands were trembling as his fingers tangled with her hair. Once again a tremor raced through his body.

"She's going to be all right," he said again.

"Thank God," Catherine whispered. She felt his heart pounding. Her breasts were flush against the hard wall of his chest, and it felt so incredibly good to be in his arms.

They might have remained like that forever if the sound from outside the room hadn't captured their attention. Even then neither one showed any inclination toward moving. Remembering all the unspoken promises they'd made to each other, Catherine gently broke away.

"Any broken bones?" was the only intelligent question she could think to ask. She ran her fingers down her cheeks, convinced her mascara was streaking her face. Using the back of her hand, she brushed the moisture aside.

"None," Royce said with a lopsided grin. "She was lucky that way. She has a bad concussion and plenty of scrapes and bruises."

"What happened?"

"One of the mothers was driving her kids to school when her brakes locked as she was coming to the school crossing. There wasn't anything she could do." Royce's eyes hardened as though he were picturing the frantic scene in his mind. The terror of the children helplessly scattering as the car slid toward them. The screams. The fear. The panic.

"Gratefully the car hit the curb before sliding into Kelly and Missy. From what I understand both were racing out of the way and were knocked hard to the ground."

"Was Kelly's friend hurt?"

"Cuts and bruises. The hospital released her to her mother."

Pressing her hands against the sides of Royce's clean-shaven jaw, Catherine closed her eyes, grateful that the accident hadn't been any worse than it was. Now that she was assured Kelly was going to be all right, she was more concerned about Royce. At one time she would have believed nothing could disconcert him, but Royce's Achilles' heel was his young daughter.

"Are you all right?"

He nodded, and offered her a weak smile. "Now that you're here, I am." He covered her hand with his own and roughly drew her palm to his mouth, tenderly kissing the inside. "Does anyone know where you are?"

Elaine Perkins had probably figured it out, but Catherine didn't want to worry Royce. "No."

"Good." His eyes were dark and intent. "Go back to the office."

"But…"

"And come back later this afternoon. Kelly will want to see you." His eyes revealed he'd want to see her again, too.

"All right," she said, reluctantly drawing away from him.

Royce reached for her hand, momentarily bringing her back to him, and pressed her fingertips to his mouth. "Thank you." He didn't need to tell her what for, it was there in his eyes for her to read. The eyes that had once seemed so hard and cold would never look the same again.

No man is an island. Royce had never completely understood those words until Kelly's accident. He'd been numb when security had come to tell him his daughter, his only child, had been taken by ambulance to the Navy Hospital. Numb with shock and disbelief. His heart had pounded so loud it sounded like a hand grenade exploding in his ears.

He hadn't said a word, but simply walked outside to his car, climbed inside and drove with a security escort to the hospital, praying, pleading with God for things to be different this time than they had been with Sandy's fatal accident.

Security Police had come to him then, too. All he'd known was that Sandy had been taken by ambulance to the Naval Hospital. The details with Kelly had been the same.

Only Sandy had been D.O.A.

Kelly had been spared.

Royce had loved his wife, at least in the beginning. He'd sensed from the first that she'd needed more love, more of him than he could ever supply. When they'd first married, the idea of being an officer's wife had excited her, but that novelty had quickly worn thin. She'd needed something more.

A career, she decided. One in which she would be appreciated and admired. One that would make her the envy of everyone she met.

Royce had encouraged her, which was his first mistake, but he hadn't expected her to become more involved with fashion than their lives together. After two years as a buyer for a major Seattle department store, she let it be known that if Royce were transferred, she'd stay behind.

In his ignorance, Royce had thought a child would help. Sandy had never been keen on raising a family. Insisting she bear him the child she'd promised was mistake number two.

After threats, tears and countless arguments, Sandy had agreed, but she'd never wanted Kelly. In some ways, Royce doubted that Sandy had ever loved their daughter.

Sandy worked up to a week before her delivery date and returned two weeks afterward. It was Royce who walked the floors when Kelly developed colic. It was Royce who dropped her off at the day-care center and returned to pick her up after work. It was Royce who changed her diapers and sat in the medical clinic when she developed repeated ear infections.

As Sandy claimed, if Royce was so keen on having a family, fine. She'd done her part.

By the time Sandy had been killed, their marriage, indeed every aspect of their relationship, had long since died a slow, painful death. They hadn't slept in the same room for three years and hadn't made love in over a year. Their lives were as separate as they could make them and still remain married.

Royce hadn't asked for a divorce. He didn't know why Sandy hadn't. They rarely spoke in those days. Rarely communicated.

Nevertheless, when she'd died, Royce had suffered. With guilt. With regret. With doubts. He should have tried harder. Done something more to make her happy. Appreciated her more. Something. Anything. Everything.

He hadn't shed a tear at her funeral. Any emotion he felt for Sandy had long since been spent. He felt guilty about that, guilty enough to promise himself he would never make the mistake of falling in love a second time.

Then he'd met Catherine.

He cursed the day she'd been assigned to his staff. In the same breath his heart swelled with gratitude.

Royce had come to believe he was a man who didn't need anyone. People needed him. Kelly needed him. The navy needed him. But he was an island, a man without needs.

He'd lived under that delusion until he'd seen Security approaching him that morning.

In that moment he'd needed Catherine. So badly that he shuddered at the memory of the way her name had raced into his mind. He'd sat in the emergency room, wanting her with him so much that he could feel himself start to unravel. A woman he felt closer to in little more than a month than he'd ever felt toward the wife he'd buried. He needed Catherine, the woman he'd never held. The woman he'd never kissed.

Royce had waited, for what seemed like hours, but in fact had only been a matter of minutes before he learned Kelly had suffered only minor injuries.

His relief had been so great that it demanded every ounce of strength he possessed not to reach for the phone and call Catherine then and there and assure her everything was all right.

His hand shook as the realization washed over him like cold November rain.

Still he wanted Catherine with him. He needed her warmth, her generosity, her support. The man who needed no one, needed her.

She must have known, must have sensed his desperation because she'd come. From out of nowhere, she'd walked into Kelly's hospital room like an apparition. When he'd first looked up and seen her standing there, Royce was convinced she wasn't real. His anguish had been so overwhelming that his troubled mind had conjured up her form to satisfy the deep craving he had for her touch.

Then her eyes had slid so hungrily to his, and she'd bit into her bottom lip and battled back the tears. Ghosts didn't cry, did they?

This one did. Somehow Royce found himself on his feet walking toward her. He half expected her to vanish when he reached for her. Instead she was warm and solid and real. And his.

Royce had been so grateful, so engulfed with gratitude that he hadn't been able to speak. His heart, which he'd taken such measures to protect, had heated with a love so strong, his throat had grown thick with emotion.

He'd held Catherine for the longest time, soaking in her strength, her love, her concern.

When he had been able to speak, he didn't

know if what he'd said was the least bit intelligible. Catherine had started asking questions; somehow he'd found the strength to answer, strength she'd lent him without even knowing it.

Then they'd heard a noise outside the room and realized their perilous position. He'd had to send her away. He'd had no choice.

"Daddy." The fragile child voice rose from the bed as delicately as mist on the moors.

"Hello, sweetheart."

"I fell asleep."

"I know." He lifted her small hand and clasped it in both of his. "You're going to be all right."

"What about Missy?"

"Her, too."

"Did I ruin my new jacket?"

How like a woman to be concerned about her clothes, Royce noted, amused. "If you did, I'll buy you another one."

Kelly brightened enough to offer him a weak smile. "I thought I heard Catherine. Did she come? I wanted to wake up and talk to her, but I couldn't. I guess I was too tired."

Royce nodded. "Don't worry, Catherine will be back later."

Kelly's soft blue eyes drifted shut, and she yawned. "Oh-h-h good, I like her so much."

"I like her, too."

Kelly's smile was lethargic. "I know you do, and she likes you a whole bunch...I can tell. Remember what I said, okay?"

"About what, sweetheart?"

"A baby sister," she reminded him, and winced. "Don't forget."

Royce hesitated. Now wasn't the time to lecture Kelly, but if she were to say anything to Catherine, it might prove extremely embarrassing. "Let me handle that part, all right?"

"All right."

Within a few minutes, Kelly was sound asleep once more.

As promised, Catherine arrived later that evening, her arms filled with a giant stuffed panda and a large vase of bright flowers.

"Catherine!" Kelly greeted. His child was sitting up in bed, looking very much like her normal self, Royce thought. The ten-year-old held out her arms as though she and the lieutenant commander were close friends.

If the truth be known, Royce was having something of a problem keeping from holding out his arms as well. Catherine looked beautiful, but then he couldn't remember a time that she'd been anything less.

Catherine set the vase of pink, red and white

carnations next to the flower arrangement Royce had brought.

"Dad said you were here earlier, but I was asleep." She hugged the panda bear and Catherine in turn. "Thank you. I didn't expect everyone to buy me gifts just because Mrs. Thompson's brakes didn't work."

"We're all so pleased you weren't hurt worse."

"It was real scary," Kelly admitted, eating up all the attention she was receiving. "I tried not to cry, but it hurt too bad."

"I probably would have cried, too," Catherine confessed. She stood across the bed from Royce, who remembered the tears in her eyes as she'd rushed into the room earlier in the day.

"Wow, what happened to this place?" Catherine said with a grin, admiring the decorations. Her gaze briefly met with Royce's and seemed almost shy.

"My teacher brought me a poster," Kelly said, pointing proudly to the large sheet of brightly decorated butcher paper. "Everyone in the class wrote me a get-well message." The ten-year-old paused. "Everyone except Eddie Reynolds. He's never forgiven me for striking him out in baseball last year." She rolled her eyes as though to say men were all fools.

"Your friends did a beautiful job."

"Did you see the flowers Dad got me and the new cassette player?"

"Yes, they're very nice."

"I almost ruined my new jacket, but Dad says all we have to do is take it to the cleaners."

"Well, you're certainly looking chipper."

"I feel real good, but the doctor said I have to stay here overnight. Dad's going to come back early in the morning and bring me home. Then tomorrow night he's going to fix my favorite dinner. Will you come, too? Dad's a real good cook, and I have so much I want to show you."

Catherine's eyes shot to Royce's. It was clear she didn't know how to answer Kelly. It was also clear, at least to Royce, that she wanted to be there just as much as he and Kelly wanted her with them.

Five

"Okay, Dad, we're ready," Kelly called out excitedly from the family room.

Catherine shared a smile with the ten-year-old as Royce wiped his hands dry on a dish towel and wandered in from the kitchen. He was busy with the dinner preparations while Catherine was keeping Kelly entertained.

"See?" Kelly held out her arms, proudly displaying her fingernails. "Aren't they gorgeous?"

As a surprise for Kelly, Catherine had brought along press-on nails, and the two had spent an hour working the dragon-length fire-engine red nails onto the girl's fingers.

"How'd you do that?" Royce blinked and seemed genuinely amazed.

"We have our ways," Catherine said, smiling up at him.

"How long before dinner?" Kelly demanded. "I'm starved. Hospital food leaves a lot to be desired, you know." She was dressed in her pajamas and sitting on the L-shaped sectional with a thick feather pillow propped at one end. According to Royce, the doctor had given instructions to keep Kelly quiet for a day or two. A feat, Catherine was quickly learning, that was easier said than done.

"Hold your horses," Royce teased. "I'm putting the finishing touches on dinner now."

"Can I help?" Catherine offered.

"I want to help, too," Kelly chimed in, tossing aside the orange, yellow and brown hand-knit afghan.

"Stay put, the both of you," Royce insisted. "The table's set. All I need to do is dish up. It'll only take me a few more minutes."

The sight of Royce working in the kitchen had done funny things to Catherine's heart. If the wardroom could only see him now! A dish towel was tucked around his waist in apron fashion, yet it did nothing to disrupt the highly charged effectiveness of his masculine appeal. The sharp edges of his character were smoothly rounded when he was with his daughter, Catherine noted. Gone was the constrained, inflexible commander who ruled with a harsh, but fair hand. Royce Nyland was said to be a man with an iron will. Indeed, Catherine had bumped against it more than once herself. He was also said to be a man with an inner core of steel, but what few realized, what few saw, was that Royce Nyland also possessed a heart of gold. A man of iron. A man of gold.

Catherine had assumed she'd feel uncomfortable in Royce's home. She wasn't entirely sure that their being together like this didn't border on an impropriety, an indiscretion that could have serious consequences for them both. But Royce had been the one who'd seconded Kelly's invitation. They'd all wanted it so badly that Catherine had thrown caution to the wind.

"Dad makes marvelous spaghetti and meat-balls," Kelly explained.

"Meat-a-balls," Royce corrected from inside the kitchen. "You can't eat Italian unless you speak it correctly. Try again."

"Meat-a-balls," Kelly returned enthusiastically. For someone who'd been hospitalized only a few hours earlier, the youngster revealed amazing vigor.

"Catherine." He pointed a sauce-coated wooden spoon in her direction.

"Meat-a-balls," she said, imitating his inflection perfectly.

"When are we going to stop talking about them and eat?" Kelly wanted to know. "I've been waiting all day for this."

"Now." Royce appeared and waved his arm toward the dining room. "Dinner is served."

The afghan on Kelly's legs went flying across the back of the sectional as she bounced to her feet. She sauntered into the dining room with her arms stretched out in front of her like a sleepwalker, her fingers splayed in an effort not to touch anything in case her nails weren't dry yet.

"Are you sure she can eat with those things?" Royce asked Catherine out of the corner of his mouth.

"I have a feeling she'll find a way."

Kelly had a problem eating at first, but once she got the hang of working her fork without her nails interfering, everything went smoothly. Although, Catherine had to admit, Kelly's first few attempts resembled something out of a Marx brothers movie.

After dinner, Catherine and Royce cleared the table and lingered over a cup of coffee in the family room.

"I can't remember when I've tasted better meat-a-balls," Catherine said, meaning it. "Kelly's right, you're an excellent cook."

Royce bowed his head, graciously accepting her compliment.

Sipping from her cup, Catherine's gaze drifted to the fireplace and the framed family photograph of Royce, Kelly and a dark-haired woman. It didn't take Catherine long to figure out the strong-featured female had been Royce's wife.

Royce's gaze followed hers. "That was taken a couple of years before the accident."

"She was beautiful."

Royce nodded, but it was clear to Catherine that the subject was a closed one. He didn't want to speak of his marriage any more than she wanted to summarize the details of her best-forgotten engagement to Aaron.

"There's a photograph on my fireplace mantel, too," she told him, struggling to keep the emotion out of her voice. She didn't often speak of her father, but she felt comfortable enough with Royce and Kelly to share this painful part of her life. When she'd finished, Catherine noted that Kelly was struggling to keep her eyes open.

"I think it's time I put her to bed," Royce whispered.

Catherine nodded, stood and took their empty coffee cups into the kitchen. Royce lifted a protesting Kelly into his arms.

"Good night, Catherine," Kelly said, covering her mouth as she yawned. When she finished, she held out her arms for a good-night hug.

Royce carried his daughter into the kitchen, and Catherine quickly gave Kelly a squeeze.

Standing that close to Royce, however, feeling him tense as her breasts brushed against his forearm, did bizarre things to her equilibrium. She had barely touched him, in the most innocent of ways, and yet her body had sprung to life with yearning.

Danger. Imaginary red lights started flashing before her eyes, and Catherine knew if Royce and she were going to maintain their platonic relationship, she was going to have to find a way to get out of his home—and fast.

Royce disappeared, and not wanting to leave him with the dishes, she quickly rinsed and stacked them in the dishwasher. She was wiping down the countertop when he reappeared.

"Leave that," he said.

"I can't," she returned quickly, her eyes avoiding him. "My mother and I had this simple rule we followed for years, and now I'm a slave to tradition."

"What was this simple rule?"

Catherine continued wiping far more vigorously than was needed. "Those who cook shouldn't have to do the dishes."

"Catherine." His voice was low and seductive. "Come here."

She swore the tension in the air between them was so thick it could be sliced and buttered. "I think it would be best if I left now, don't you?"

Slowly she raised her eyes to his, seeking confirmation.

"No, I don't." He said so much more in those few simple words. He told her he was weary of this constant tension between them. He was through waiting. His patience had reached its endurance level. So had hers, and he knew it. She wanted this, too. Sweet heaven how she wanted it.

Silence swelled between them, but for the first time in recent memory it was a comfortable silence unencumbered with misgivings and uncertainties. They both knew they were unwilling to wait any longer.

Royce took her by the hand and led her to the sectional sofa recently vacated by Kelly, pulling her down so they were side by side. They didn't speak, but there was no need for words, indeed words would have been a drawback.

Royce held her head between his hands and carefully studied her face. The look in his eyes, so earnest and intense, humbled her. They said she was the most beautiful woman in the world. His woman. Catherine wasn't going to argue with him, although she wasn't nearly as beautiful as he seemed to believe. His eyes smoldered with a blue light of yearning. Catherine was convinced his look was a reflection of her own. There was nothing between them. No pretense. No qualms. Only need. A need so honest, so comfortable, it seemed to flow between them like the peaceful waters of a rolling river.

Royce's mouth made a slow descent, and with a sigh, Catherine closed her eyes and raised her chin to be rewarded with what she'd waited so long to receive.

Catherine thought she was prepared. How wrong she was. How ill equipped. The moment his mouth met hers, she was assaulted with a swarm of warm sensations that came at her with the force of a bulldozer. He was gentle, so gentle. She hadn't expected that. Not when the hunger was so wild. Not when she'd been smothered in sensation long before his mouth found hers.

Catherine was enveloped in tenderness. She'd known from the first that Royce's kiss would be special; she hadn't expected to feel sensations so unbelievably potent that tears crowded the edges of her eyes. Sensations so powerful it was as though she'd never felt anything before this moment.

Royce groaned and slipped his mouth from hers. Burying his face in her hair, he drew in a deep, shuddering breath. He was about to speak, but she intercepted his action by directing his lips back to hers. They both seemed ready this time, prepared to deal with the wealth of sensation, eager to accept it. His tongue sought hers; she met his eagerly with soft, welcoming touches.

They found a rhythm with each other. A cadence. It was as though they were familiar lovers, enjoying a long series of deep, lengthy kisses full of hunger and desperate need. Soon Catherine was clinging mindlessly to Royce. Prepared for anything, for everything.

"I knew it would be like this." He braced his forehead against hers as he drew in several deep, even breaths as though he were struggling to believe all that was between them.

Catherine hadn't known it would be anything close to this wonderful. She hadn't a clue. Nothing could have prepared her for the fierce onslaught of feelings. Her body pulsed with desire, a need so great that she hurt in strange places.

Royce's hands shook slightly as he unfastened the buttons of her gray silk blouse. He peeled it open and released the clasp of her bra, then caught her breasts in his open palms as they sprang free.

Catherine moaned at the fresh onslaught of warm sensations. Her nipples were hard long before Royce caressed them with the callused pads of his thumbs. She thought it impossible, but they tightened even more. The feelings were unfamiliar, this being so needy, so wanting.

Slowly he lowered his mouth to the summit

of her breast, capturing the tender nipple between his lips, laving it with the rough edges of his tongue. When Catherine was convinced she could endure no more, he drew it into his mouth and sucked gently. Catherine moaned and buried her fingers in his short hair, needing to touch him. She felt so close to him, closer than she had to anyone. She loved him so much in that moment, it was all she could do not to weep. Royce loved her, too. Catherine was as confident of that as she was of his love for Kelly.

Royce transferred his attention to her other breast, and Catherine groaned once more. She recognized the sound. It was the type of whimpering noise a woman makes when she's ready to make love, ready to receive a man.

Royce apparently recognized it too, and slowly raised his head. His gaze melded with hers, seeking confirmation.

Catherine's heart was in her throat. She wanted him. He wanted her. Oh, sweet heaven, how she wanted him. Royce must have read the need in her eyes and, responding to it, reached for her once more, his hands cupping the undersides of her face.

His mouth found hers in a hot kiss of savage frenzy. He thrust his tongue forward and swept her mouth with a wild kiss that told her he was fast reaching the point of no return. Even as he kissed her, his hands dropped to work open the zipper in the jut of her hip.

Some shred of reasoning, some ray of sanity grasped hold of Catherine's mind before Royce managed to succeed in opening her slacks. Had they both gone crazy? With their very careers on the line, they'd walked into this with their eyes wide open. In one blindingly clear revelation, Catherine knew they had to stop. It wasn't what she wanted. It wasn't what Royce wanted, either. But it was necessary.

"Royce...no." She scrambled from the sectional, her chest heaving with the effort. She had to escape before it was too late, before he kissed her again.

"Catherine?" Her name became a mixture of shock and need. "What's wrong?"

"Nothing," she assured him, so close to tears her voice wobbled like a toy top. "Everything," she amended. She couldn't stand so close to him and not be affected. It was either move away or fall willingly back into his arms. She couldn't resist him; she couldn't think when he was looking at her with such tenderness and concern.

She moved across the room from him, and braced herself against the opposite wall, needing its support. Her heart was beating so hard, the sound ricocheted around the room, each beat stronger, each beat louder. Surely Royce could hear. Surely he knew.

"We can't do it…we can't," she whispered, fighting back the tears. "Don't you understand how foolish it would be for us both…"

Royce moved off the sofa and walked purposely toward her. "Why not? Kelly's upstairs asleep…."

"Please, oh, please, don't argue with me. This is hard enough…so hard." Explaining would have depleted her of the strength she needed to follow through with her resolve.

Capturing her hands in his own, Royce lifted them above her head, and then, leaning forward, boxed her in with his muscled arms. His body was so close, she could feel the heat radiating off him.

"Royce," she pleaded once again, rolling her head to one side.

His thighs, taut and hard, pressed against her. It wasn't the only part of his anatomy that was hard, and that was pressed against her as well. Catherine moaned as the excitement shuddered through her, and dropped her head, weakening. It would be so easy to swirl her hips, to move against him. She longed to savor his strength, his power. It would be so easy to surrender to the gnawing need.

"Royce, what?" His mouth was so close, so

warm. He nudged his nose against her earlobe, then took it gently between his teeth and sucked. Once again wild excitement seized her, and it was all she could do to keep from buckling against him.

"Don't…oh, please, don't." But her pleas lacked conviction. If anything they sounded more like a siren's call, an inducement to continue doing the very things he was.

"You taste so sweet," he murmured, dragging his mouth down the slope of her neck, then taking nibbling kisses at the scented hollow of her throat. Catherine moaned and rotated her head, granting him access to his desires. And he did desire her. It was as if a giant storehouse of need had been building in both of them, and had burst open all at once.

His mouth found hers, his kisses hot, filled with an untamed urgency, his hunger as raw as her own. His tongue swept her mouth, and before she realized what she was doing, Catherine pulled her hands free from his and grabbed at his shirt, demanding more and more, holding on. Royce answered by ravishing her mouth in a kiss so blistering, so carnal that any and all resistance in Catherine melted.

Pinning her against the wall with his hips, Royce started to move against her. Their kisses were so fiery, the air sizzled. The night sizzled. They sizzled.

Abruptly Royce dragged his mouth from hers. "Tell me you want this as much as I do," he whispered. His voice was thick and hot. So hot against her skin his breath alone was enough to scorch her.

That Royce would need her assurance touched something deep within Catherine. "Oh, Royce, yes…only…"

"What?"

"Only I won't be able to hide the way I feel if we make love. Not from anyone." Monday morning Elaine Perkins would guess what had happened between her and Royce. Catherine didn't doubt it for a moment. "I'm not nearly as good at disguising my feelings as you. It's hard enough now, but if we make love…if we do this… Everyone will know."

Royce went still for several heart-stopping moments before making a low, guttural sound of frustration and defeat. His shoulders heaved once as he rolled away from her and pressed his own back against the wall. "You're right."

"If I'm so right, then why is it so damned hard?"

"I don't know." He spoke through gritted teeth as he reined in his desire.

Catherine felt like weeping. "What are we going to do?"

Royce expelled his breath forcefully. "The hell if I know. I just hope to God the Navy appreciates this." Straightening, he heaved in one giant breath, squared his shoulders and with some effort managed to snap her bra closed. Then with deliberate businesslike movements he fastened her blouse, kissed her one last time sweetly, gently and whispered, "Now go, before I change my mind."

"Morning, Dad," Kelly said as she walked into the kitchen, dressed in her housecoat and slippers. She pulled out the chair and reached for a section of the Sunday paper. "What time did Catherine go home last night?"

"Early." Too damn early, Royce mused. Unfortunately it hadn't been soon enough. Royce couldn't believe how far matters had developed the night before. How far he'd *let* them develop. He'd never been closer to defying Navy regulations. If the commanding officer were to learn he was having an affair with Catherine Fredrickson, their lives would be ruined. Royce had seen it once before. An acquaintance had fallen in love with a woman in his command. They'd been discreet, or so they believed. Eventually it was discovered and they were investigated. No allowances had been made. No leeway given. Both parties involved had been immediately court-martialed.

Royce didn't know what the hell he'd been thinking. That was just it. He *wasn't* thinking. Thank God Catherine had the presence of mind to call an end to matters when she had. She was right. If they made love, neither one of them would have been able to continue with the pretense. True, Catherine was far more readable than he was, but Royce knew himself well enough to recognize there would be problems with him, too. Major problems.

"Can I call Catherine?" Kelly asked, reaching across the table for the comics.

"I don't think that would be a good idea."

"Why not?"

Royce wasn't in any mood to argue with his daughter, and his voice was sharp when he spoke. "Because I said you couldn't. I don't want any arguments about this, Kelly. Catherine is off limits." To them both, unfortunately.

Kelly gave him an indignant look, scooted out of her chair and stalked out of the kitchen. Just before she reached the doorway, she bolted around and glared at him. "Sometimes you're an unreasonable grouch."

If Kelly thought he was bad now, give him another six months of working side by side with

Catherine, knowing he'd never be able to hold her or kiss her again.

"What's with Commander Nyland?" Elaine Perkins questioned when Catherine returned from a session in court early Friday afternoon. Catherine had been in and out of the office all week acting as prosecutor on a series of criminal trials. If Royce's mood had been anything other than normal, she hadn't noticed.

"What's wrong?" she asked, setting a load of files down on her desk.

"If I knew that I wouldn't be asking you. He's been in a bad mood all week, making unreasonable demands on himself and everyone else. You would think once he found out his daughter wasn't badly hurt he'd be in a good mood. If anything it's gotten worse."

"If Commander Nyland has a problem, trust me, he isn't going to share it with me." Catherine did her best to maintain the pretense that she and Royce did nothing more than work together. She hadn't talked to him outside the office all week. The fact didn't trouble her; they both needed distance to put order to their thoughts.

Now that she thought about it, Catherine was willing to admit that Elaine did have a point. Royce seemed to be putting in plenty of hours, making too many demands on himself and consequently everyone else. He'd never gone out for any personality awards, nor was he in a popularity contest. If that were the case he'd lose hands down.

A couple of the other clerks rolled back their chairs. "Ever read much about arctic seals, Lieutenant Commander?" Elaine Perkins asked as the others slowly gathered around the secretary's desk.

"No." Catherine wondered what the men were up to.

"Apparently when danger is near they gather on a floating iceberg. The problem is they don't know when the danger has passed and so a sacrificial seal is thrown into the water. If he survives the others know it's safe to leave the iceberg."

Catherine stared at the small party of men gathered around Elaine's desk. A couple had leaned forward, pressing their hands to her desktop. "So?" Catherine demanded, not liking the sounds of this.

"We just voted you to be our sacrificial seal."

"What?" If she hadn't been so amused, she might have been concerned. Apparently she hadn't done as good a job as she'd hoped, hiding her feelings for Royce. The staff seemed to think she had some influence with their XO. A dangerous sign.

"It makes sense for you to be the one to approach him," Elaine explained before Catherine could ask why they'd bestowed the dubious honor upon her. "Commander Nyland may have all the sensitivity of seaweed, but he's still a man, and as such he's as susceptible as the rest of us to a pretty face."

"And what exactly am I supposed to say to him?"

"I don't have a clue. You're supposed to figure that out yourself. Just do whatever it is you do to put a man into a better mood."

"Please do it soon," Seaman Webster added. "I've had to type the same paper five times. He wants it perfect. The last time I had a comma out of place, and you would have thought the free world was in jeopardy."

"Sorry, fellows," Catherine said, walking back into her office, ignoring them as much as possible. She was staying away from this situation with Royce with a ten-foot pole. "You picked the wrong lady to do your dirty work for you. If Commander Nyland's in a foul mood, you'll ride it out together the way you always have. Furthermore I find your attitude highly chauvinistic."

"Oh, I agree," Elaine Perkins commented. "But we're desperate."

"I said no," she returned crisply. "And I mean it."

There was a fair amount of grumbling, but the staff gradually returned to their desks. Elaine Perkins, however, continued to study Catherine. "I thought you and the commander were friends."

"We are," Catherine said, doing her best to keep her tone light and unaffected.

"I understood that the two of you jogged together most afternoons."

Catherine wondered when she'd heard that and from whom. "Not anymore. I usually run in the mornings."

"Damn. I was hoping you might be able to talk to him casually some afternoon, find out what's bugging him. There isn't any need to make the rest of us suffer just because he's unhappy about something."

"Are you suffering, Mrs. Perkins?" Royce demanded from behind Catherine's secretary in a voice so cold, the words froze in midair.

Elaine went pale. "No, sir," she answered briskly.

"I'm glad to hear it." He hesitated long enough to look toward Catherine. "I'd like the Ellison report on my desk before you leave tonight."

"Yes, sir," Catherine returned just as crisply. She was hours from being anywhere close to finishing the report. Royce must have known it. Apparently she, too, was to receive the brunt of his foul mood, but then why should she be different from anyone else?

With that, Royce returned to his office and closed the door.

Elaine slumped back into her chair and released her breath in a slow exercise. "He wants you to have that report done by tonight?" she moaned.

"Don't worry, it won't take me long." Longer than she would have liked, but that couldn't be helped.

"Do you want me to stay and type it up for you?"

Catherine appreciated the offer, but it wasn't necessary. "No, thanks, it won't take me long."

"Aren't you furious with him?" Elaine asked under her breath, her gaze leveled on the closed door that led to Royce's office.

"No." Maybe she should be, but Catherine had learned long before that Royce's bark was far worse than his bite. She said as much to Elaine.

"Right, but you don't seem to be the one he's biting all the time."

The humor drained out of Catherine. The

more she thought about Elaine's comment, the more concerned she became. Was it true? Had Royce given her more slack than the other members of his staff? Apparently they'd all felt the brunt of his bad mood in the past several days. But if what Elaine Perkins said was true, something had to be done, and quickly.

Catherine waited until later that same afternoon when Royce went down to the track. She gave him enough time to run several laps before she joined him. He looked over at her and frowned, his look so dark and uninviting that a shiver of apprehension moved over her. "The Ellison report is on your desk."

"Is there a problem?" He hadn't decreased his speed any, and she was having a problem maintaining his pace.

"Ah...ever hear of a sacrificial seal?"

"I beg your pardon?"

"Nothing...forget I said that."

They ran half a lap, then he turned to stare at her again. His eyes were cold, his look detached. That should have pleased her, should have assured her Elaine was imagining things, but it didn't. "We might have a problem."

"Is that a fact, Lieutenant Commander? Thank you so much for taking it upon yourself to inform me of this."

"More than...the usual problem."

"And what, tell me, is the *usual* problem?"

"There isn't any need to be so damned sarcastic," she said, affronted by his attitude.

"Isn't there?" he returned. "What do I have to do, order you off this track? I thought I'd made myself clear about the subject of us jogging together."

"You did, but..."

"Then kindly respect my wishes."

The wall was back in place, so firmly erected that Catherine was left to wonder if everything that had blossomed between them was a figment of her imagination. Royce was so cold. So caustic.

"What about my wishes?" she asked softly.

Royce came to an abrupt halt. His blue eyes had never been more piercing. "Listen, Lieutenant Commander, you have no wishes. If you didn't learn that early in your Navy career then we have a real problem. I'm your executive officer. You will do what I say, when I say it, without question. Is that understood?"

Catherine swallowed back a cry of protest. She blinked and nodded. "Yes, sir."

"Good. Now stay off this track from five o'clock on." He made it sound like a direct order, when in fact he had no right to tell her when she could or couldn't be on the track.

"Is that clear?" he demanded.

"Very clear, sir." The "sir" was shouted.

"Good." There was no regret in his voice. No emotion. Only a wall so high and so thick, Catherine doubted she'd ever be able to scale its heights again.

Six

The phone was ringing when Catherine let herself into her apartment Saturday afternoon. Setting the bag of groceries on the kitchen counter and ignoring Sambo's protest over being ignored, she lurched for the receiver.

"Hello," she said, fighting breathlessness.

"Hi." It was Kelly, that much Catherine could tell, but it sounded like Royce's daughter was talking with her head inside a bucket.

"Kelly?"

"Yeah, it's me."

"What's wrong?"

"Nothing. It's just that I'm not supposed to be calling you, and if Dad finds out I'm in big trouble. I've got the phone cord stretched into the closet and I'm whispering as loud as I can. Can you hear me all right?"

"Just barely. Now tell me what's up." Catherine did her best to ignore the pain of Royce's most recent order.

"You still like me and my Dad, don't you?"

"Oh, yes, sweetheart, of course I do." But it was more complicated than that, and Catherine couldn't allow the youngster to go on thinking matters could continue the way they had. "There are problems, though."

"I know, Dad explained everything to me." Kelly paused, and Catherine could hear the frustration and disappointment hum over the telephone wire with every word the youngster spoke. "Sometimes I hate the Navy."

"Don't," Catherine pleaded softly. "Those rules were made for a very good reason."

"But Dad said we couldn't have you over to the house anymore and that we couldn't go to the movies or go out to dinner or things like that. He said it would be best if I forgot all about you because that was what he was going to do."

Kelly's words went through Catherine like a steel point. The pain was so sharp and so real that she swallowed hard and bit her lower lip.

"I don't want to forget about you," the ten-year-old whispered, her voice trembling as if she were close to tears, "I kept thinking that Dad and you…that you might be my mom someday. I asked God to send me a mom, especially one with pretty fingernails, and then Dad met you and he was listening to me when I asked him about getting me a baby sister and then all of a sudden..."

"And now everything looks so bad. I won't forget you, sweetheart, and the Navy doesn't have anything to say about the two of us being special friends."

"It doesn't?"

"Not in the least. We'll give your dad and me time to work matters out at the office, and once everything is settled there, I'll invite you over for the night and we can order pizza and rent a movie and we'll do our fingernails."

"Oh, Catherine, could we really? I'd like that so much."

"I'd like that, too."

There was a bit of commotion behind Kelly that sounded like a door being jerked opened. "I've got to go now, *Missy*," Kelly said deliberately loud, placing heavy emphasis on her friend's name.

"I take it your dad just opened the closet door?" Catherine asked, unable to contain a smile.

"Right."

"All right, sweetheart. Now listen, it probably would be best if you didn't phone me again for a while. But I promise I'll talk to your dad..."

"Only do it soon, okay?" she pleaded.

"I will, I promise," Catherine pledged, feeling more depressed than ever.

The despair had grown heavier and more oppressive a week later. Royce hadn't spoken one unnecessary word to her in all that time. It was as though she were invisible. A necessary body that filled a space. Necessary to the legal department, but not necessary for him. If Royce did happen to glance in her direction it was by accident, and it seemed he looked straight through her.

The weekend hadn't been much better. Catherine couldn't remember a Saturday and Sunday that felt more empty. On Saturday she'd done busywork around her apartment and answered mail. At least her good friend Brand Davis from Hawaii was happy, she mulled, reading over the wedding invitation. Then on Sunday, after church services, she'd attended a matinee and cooked a meal she didn't feel like eating, and ended up giving the leftovers to Sambo, who apparently wasn't interested, either.

Outwardly everything was as it always had been, but inside Catherine felt empty. As empty as a black hole. How stark her life felt, how barren. Until she'd met Royce, she'd been blissfully unaware of the lonely nothingness of her life. Royce had stirred her soul to life, and now she hungered for someone to share the everyday routine, someone to give meaning to her bleak existence.

The single red rose in a crystal stem vase was sitting on her desk waiting for her when she walked into the office Monday morning. Her heart quickened at the beauty of the delicate flower, but she knew immediately it couldn't, wouldn't be from Royce. He wasn't a man who would allow a rose to do his speaking for him. He wasn't a man to indulge in such romantic extravagances.

A card was pinned to the shiny red ribbon attached to the narrow vase. Catherine stared at the envelope for several moments, calculating in her mind who would have given her a rose.

"Aren't you going to read who it's from?" Elaine asked, much too casually to fool Catherine.

"In time." She unpinned the card and slipped it free of the small envelope. The name was scrawled across the face of the card in bold, even strokes. She grinned, somewhat amused. It was exactly who she thought it would be. Knowing Elaine was watching her, she replaced the card in the envelope, then set the rose on the edge of her desk.

"Well?" Elaine demanded impatiently. "Who sent it?"

"My, my, aren't you the nosy one?"

"If you must know, it's a little more than idle curiosity."

Catherine pulled out her chair and sat down. "I suppose you've got money riding on this."

"Ten bucks." Then without hesitation, she asked, "Commander Parker, right?"

Catherine grinned and nodded.

"I knew it all along," Elaine said, grinning broadly.

Catherine was pleased her secretary took such delight in the fact Commander Dan Parker had seen fit to flatter her with a red rose, but frankly, her secretary was more thrilled about it than she was.

Her lack of appreciation, Catherine realized, could be attributed to the fact she realized what was sure to follow. An invitation she didn't want to accept. It happened just as she suspected, just when she was preparing to leave the office that same afternoon. Commander Parker strolled into the room, grinning boyishly.

"Good afternoon, Catherine," he greeted, and struck a casual pose. He was tall and reasonably good-looking, his features well defined. From the scuttlebutt Catherine had picked up around the base, Dan Parker had the reputation of being a playboy.

"Good afternoon, Commander," she re-

sponded formally, wanting to keep it impersonal.

His gaze drifted over to her desk, where she'd
left the rose. "I see you found my little surprise."

"It was very thoughtful of you," she said, eye-
ing the door, anxious to get away. The office
was deserted, and she didn't want to get stuck
in a long, boring conversation with a man she
had no interest in cultivating a relationship with.

"I'm pleased you enjoyed it so much."

"It's lovely." She reached for her coat and
slipped into it, doing her best to give the appearance that she was about to leave. Anything
that would cut short this game of cat and mouse.

Commander Parker would ask her out, and
she'd decline. Then he'd give her his well-
practiced hurt-little-boy look, and she'd be required to spend the next ten minutes making
up some excuse why she wouldn't go out with
him. Something that would soothe the ruffled
feathers of his substantial male ego.

"I don't suppose you have plans Friday
night?" he asked right on cue.

"Sorry, I'm busy." Which was true. She
planned on changing Sambo's litter box. Not
exactly an exciting prospect, but it gave cre-
dence to her words. She looped the strap of her
purse over her shoulder, determined not to play
the game.

"I was hoping you'd let me take you to dinner."

"Another time perhaps," she suggested, heading toward the door.

"What about the Birthday Ball?" Every October the Navy celebrated its birthday with an elaborate ball. The celebration was coming later this year because the admiral had been gone. "It's two weeks away, and I was hoping you'd accompany me."

Catherine didn't have a single excuse. Her presence would be expected, but she hadn't given the matter of a date more than a fleeting thought.

The idea of spending the evening with anyone other than Royce didn't interest her. Her attitude was excessively stupid. They'd be able to dance once, maybe twice without raising suspicions. Risking anything more than that would be foolish in the extreme. The way matters were between them presently, it was doubtful Royce would go anywhere near her.

"Catherine," Dan prodded. "The Birthday Ball?"

She forced herself to smile as though it was a difficult decision. "I appreciate the invitation, in fact I'm flattered, but no thanks. I'm...I've decided to go stag this year. It's nothing personal, Dan."

Commander Parker's smile didn't waver, neither did the light in his dark eyes dim, if anything it brightened. Slowly, without hesitation, he raised his hand and ran one finger down the side of her cheek. "I think I know why."

Catherine's heart thundered against her chest with alarm. She stared up at him and blinked, certain he could read everything she felt for Royce like a notice on a bulletin board.

"Don't worry," he whispered sympathetically, "your secret is safe with me."

Squaring her shoulders, Catherine's only choice was to pretend he couldn't be more wrong. "I don't know what you're talking about. I prefer to attend the Birthday Ball alone this year, and whatever connotation you put on that decision is of your own making."

Dan chuckled. "You're right, of course. Absolutely right." He straightened and was about to leave when he turned back, his friendly eyes suddenly somber and dark. "Good luck, Catherine, but be careful. Understand?"

Before she could continue with the pretense, Catherine nodded. "I will."

Royce was in a foul mood, but that wasn't anything new. He'd been in a dangerous one for nearly two weeks, and frankly he couldn't see it lessening anytime soon. The fact he'd recently spoken to Dan Parker hadn't improved his disposition any. Of all the foolish, mule-headed deeds Catherine had committed since he'd met her, rejecting Dan's invitation to the Birthday Ball took the cake. He'd like to wring her skinny neck.

"Ha," he said aloud, discrediting his thoughts. The last thing he wanted was to see Catherine suffer. Anytime he was within ten feet of her it was all he could do not to haul her into his arms and breathe in the fresh, womanly scent that was hers alone. He wanted to drink in her softness, savor her warmth and her love. He needed her so damn much, he was about to go out of his mind.

Royce didn't know what the hell he was going to do. One thing for sure, they couldn't continue like this much longer.

Royce had done everything he could think to do to forget her. He was working himself into an early grave, spending all kinds of extra hours at the office. Kelly was barely speaking to him, and he'd lost just about every friend he'd made in seventeen years of military service.

Something had to be done, and fast, before he ended up destroying himself and in the process, Catherine, too. He just didn't know what the hell the solution was.

A polite knock on his door interrupted his

thoughts. Whoever it was possessed the courage of David facing Goliath to confront Royce in his current mood.

"Come in," he barked.

When Catherine opened the door, Royce's heart dropped to his knees. What now? He couldn't be any less encouraging than the last time they spoke. He couldn't have been any more sarcastic. No matter what he said, no matter what he did, she just kept coming back. By heaven, that woman was stubborn.

"Yes?" he demanded, giving the illusion of being busy, too busy to be intruded upon.

"I need to talk to you."

How sweet her voice sounded, how soft and feminine. Royce had lain awake nights tormented by the memory of her making delicate, whimpering love sounds. How close he'd come to breaking the very code of honor he'd sworn to uphold.

"There's nothing more to say," he said, forcefully pushing all thoughts of her and that night from his mind. "I thought I made that fact perfectly clear." His voice was as brittle and hard as he could make it.

"It's about Kelly."

"My daughter is none of your business, Lieutenant Commander." Royce felt as though he'd been kicked in the stomach. Catherine had no way of knowing that Kelly continued to bring up her name night and day until he'd absolutely forbidden his own daughter to speak of her.

"If you have no objection, I'd like Kelly to spend the weekend with me and…"

"No." The word was edged with steel.

"Wanting to spend time with Kelly has nothing to do with you and me," Catherine insisted softly. "But everything to do with Kelly. She needs…"

"I'll be the one to determine my daughter's needs."

The silence between them stretched to ear-splitting proportions. Royce half expected the window glass to shatter under the pressure. Neither spoke. Neither daring. Neither willing to give an inch.

Royce feared an inch would soon lead to two and three, and before he could stop himself, he and Catherine would become lovers. The very word brought a tight hardening to his loins. It didn't take much for his tormented mind to envision her soft and willing beneath him, opening her life and her heart to him. The ache grew worse, but he wasn't sure which hurt worse: the pain in his loins, or the one in his heart.

"I understand you turned down Commander Parker's invitation to the Birthday Ball," he said when it became apparent she was going to continue with the same argument. His best tactic, he decided, was to change the subject.

"How'd you know that?" she asked, her beautiful dark eyes narrowing.

"Dan told me."

"Like hell, he did," she flared. "Commander Parker is a typical man. He isn't likely to tell anyone I refused his offer unless he was asked and…" She paused, and a deep shade of red seeped steadily up her neck and invaded her cheeks. "You…you asked him to invite me, didn't you?" She made it sound as though he'd attempted to involve her in treason. "You went to Dan and encouraged him to take me to…to the Birthday Ball." She closed her eyes momentarily, as though mortified to the very marrow of her bones.

"Listen, Catherine…"

Leaning forward, she pressed her hands against the side of his desk. "How dare you."

"You're out of order here, Lieutenant Commander." Royce could see he was digging himself in deeper than he intended. The most expedient way of extracting himself was to pull rank. Not the wisest means, but the most practical.

She ignored him as she straightened, then started pacing the length of his office, her steps clipped and angry. "You have one hell of a nerve, Royce. What makes you think you can rule my life?"

"Our discussion is over." He reached for his pen and commenced writing. He didn't know if a single word was legible, but that wasn't the point. Catherine, her eyes bright with unshed tears, stared at him with her heart on her sleeve. He had to get her out of his office before he did something foolish. Before he succumbed to what would, in the end, destroy them both.

"Why?" she asked. The lone word was saturated with emotion.

"You know the answer to that," he informed her stiffly, fighting back the urge to shout at her. She wasn't stupid; surely she could figure out his motives on her own.

"You honestly think it would help if I were to become involved with Dan?" Her words were low and disbelieving. When he didn't answer right away, she raised her voice. "Do you?"

"This discussion would be better left for another time," Royce informed her in his best military voice. "You may leave now." This was the tone he used often, expecting immediate and unquestioned compliance to his words.

"No way," she said, then stalked across the room and slammed closed the door, although they both knew they were alone. "We won't discuss this another time, because we're going to have this out here and now."

Royce bolted to his feet, as angry now as she. "If you value your commission, Lieutenant Commander, then I suggest you do as I ask."

She didn't so much as blink. "What exactly have you *asked?* That I date Commander Parker?"

"It certainly wouldn't hurt matters any," he said pointedly.

She knotted her fist at her side, and Royce had the impression she did so in an effort to hold on to her anger, and it required both hands.

"It may come as something of a surprise to you, Commander Nyland, but it's none of the Navy's business whom I date. It most certainly isn't any of yours!"

"In this case it is." Royce amazed himself by remaining calm, at least on the outside. Inside, he was a mess, something he wasn't willing to admit often, but Catherine had driven him to the outer edges of sanity.

"What makes you think dating Dan would help either of us? Answer me! I'm downright curious."

"Just do it, Catherine, for both our sakes."

"No," she cried, "if you want me out of your life, that's your business, but I refuse to make it easy for you."

A tear rolled down the side of her face, her precious sweet face, and it was all Royce could do not to reach out and comfort her. He slumped back in his chair and rammed all ten fingers through his hair in an urgent effort to regain control of himself. Shouting at each other wasn't going to accomplish anything. Neither was pretending.

"Sit down, Catherine," he instructed, motioning toward the chair.

"I prefer to stand." She was as stiff as plastic, eyes focused straight ahead. The evidence of that lone tear or any others had long since vanished.

"Fine. Have it your way." The fight was out of him, and he leaned back in his chair and braced his index fingers beneath his chin the way he did when he needed to think. "You were right," he stated after a while.

She blinked as though she wasn't sure she'd heard him correctly. "About what?"

"About what would happen if we'd made love that night."

Catherine's eyes briefly found his. "Even if everyone in the entire office hadn't guessed afterward, it would have been wrong."

"Only because the rule book claims it is," she argued. Her look told him the love between them was right, and always would be, no matter what the Navy decreed.

"No," he argued, gaining conviction. "Don't you understand? Can't you see? That night would have only been the beginning. Once we crossed the physical boundaries, there'd be no going back for either of us."

"I agree, but that doesn't make it wrong."

"We'd live in constant fear of being discovered, of someone, anyone finding out the truth," he continued with conviction. "We'd both make an effort, but it wouldn't be long before we'd be so desperate for each other that we'd be meeting in out-of-the-way spots—"

"We wouldn't," she cried, shaking her head in denial.

"Renting cheap hotel rooms," he added, and cringed inwardly at the thought. Catherine was too much a lady for clandestine meetings in dirty rooms. An affair would destroy the warm, generous woman he'd come to love. An affair would destroy them both. What had started out so pure and good would become tarnished and ugly. In the end it would devastate them both. He loved her too much to put her through that kind of heartache.

"No," she cried a second time, "we wouldn't let it go that far."

"Do you honestly think we'd be able to stop? Do you?" he demanded.

Catherine had gone terribly pale, so pale that Royce was tempted to take her by the hand and lead her to a chair before she collapsed. He was grateful when she chose to sit of her own accord.

"What about your transfer?" she asked, lifting her eyes to his.

Her gentle pleading was back, and it cut deep at his heart to deny her anything. If he had received the NATO assignment, although it meant they'd be separated by thousands of miles, the Navy restrictions would no longer apply.

"What I heard was a rumor," he reminded her, "nothing more. It's not going to happen." Kelly would be able to remain with him, but the blessings were mixed ones. His life with his daughter would go on without disruption, but he was going to be forced to drive the woman he loved out of his life.

"I see," she murmured, her words layered with defeat.

"What happened that Saturday night was entirely my fault." Royce felt he should admit that much. "I was so sure I was going to receive that transfer that I let matters go too far. Way too far. Monday morning I learned Commander Wayne

Nelson out of San Diego had been given the assignment."

"It isn't necessary to assign blame."

In theory Royce agreed with her, but he wanted to accept the responsibility. He'd felt so close to Catherine that evening. Closer than he had to anyone ever. They'd kissed, and the sensation had struck him as powerfully as a bolt of lightning. It seemed melodramatic to compare her touch with the forces of nature, but Royce could think of no other way to describe it. His skin had felt branded by her gentleness, and his heart…his heart had swollen with a love so strong it left him weak and trembling. He'd never desired a woman more than he had Catherine that night.

It wasn't until later, after Royce learned that the NATO assignment had gone to an acquaintance of his, that he realized his mistake. He'd lowered his guard, allowed to happen what he'd promised himself never would. As a result, he was faced with an even more difficult problem than before.

"What about Kelly?" Catherine asked, her voice so thin he could barely hear her. Slowly she raised those same pleading eyes to his. She seemed to be saying how unfair it was to punish the little girl for something that was beyond Kelly's control.

Royce had learned early in life that the book on fair had yet to be written. He wanted to do what was right for his daughter, but he couldn't do or say anything that would mislead the ten-year-old into thinking there could be a relationship between him and Catherine.

"It's a delicate situation, and best left alone," he said reluctantly.

"No," Catherine argued with surprising strength. "I won't let you do it. I won't use Kelly…you have my word on that—but she needs a woman just now, and I…I seem to be the one she's reaching out to. Please, Royce…"

He hesitated. Saying no to Catherine was as difficult as refusing his own flesh and blood. "All right," he agreed, praying he was doing the right thing.

"We sat up all night and talked and talked and talked, and Catherine painted my toenails and she even let me paint hers."

"So you had a good time?"

"The best." Kelly squeezed him tight around the stomach. Friday night and all day Saturday the house had been as quiet as a tomb. Royce had aimlessly walked around feeling lost and alone. Kelly had spent the night with friends before, and he'd never felt as he had this time. This particular aloneness. Perhaps it was because he'd wanted to be with Catherine so much himself.

By noon, he found himself glancing at the clock every five minutes. When Catherine dropped Kelly off around three, it was all he could do not to run outside and greet her. Only it wasn't Kelly he was so eager to see.

It was Catherine.

Hell, he'd been a fool to think this was going to work.

"...I don't think she's feeling very well, though."

Royce heard the tail end of his daughter's comment as she blurted out the details of each and every minute she and Catherine had been together.

"What makes you say that?" Royce asked, trying to hide his concern behind a casual facade.

"We went shopping, and then...oh," Kelly cried excitedly, "I nearly forgot to show you, Catherine bought me a surprise. Just a minute and I'll go get it." Before he could divert Kelly back to his original question, she was racing up the stairs. Two minutes later, she returned wearing a pair of hot pink earmuffs. She put them on her head, then twirled around to show him the full effect.

"Aren't they cute?"

"Beautiful. Now what makes you think Catherine isn't feeling well?" Gone was the carefully concealed apprehension.

"Oh." Kelly frowned and removed the earmuffs. "After lunch we went out for Mexican food and Catherine ordered a chili something…"

"That explains it," Royce teased.

"No. She wasn't feeling bad until she got her mail. I think it had something to do with that. She opened a letter, and the next thing I knew she was staring out the window, looking real spacey. I think she might have been crying, but when I asked her, she said she had something in her eye."

The gutsy woman Royce knew wouldn't easily give in to tears unless something was drastically wrong.

Kelly hesitated. "I think she was crying, though…I don't know. Catherine's not the type to let on about that sort of thing."

"What happened next?" he pressed, losing patience.

"Well, she made herself a cup of tea and said it was time to run me home. I didn't want to come back so soon, but I didn't say so because I knew she wanted to be alone."

"How did things go on the ride home?" Royce was beginning to feel like a detective, ferreting out each bit of information he could.

"She was real quiet. That's why I think she's not feeling very good."

Catherine was on Royce's mind for the remainder of the day. Hell, what was so unusual about that, he asked himself as he turned out the lights before heading up to bed. The beautiful Lieutenant Commander was in his mind about ninety-nine percent of the time, despite his best efforts to forget about her. Having Kelly chatter about her for hours on end certainly didn't help matters any.

Royce swore the kid had talked nonstop from the moment Catherine had let her off at the door. She'd repeated everything two and three times, so excited about every detail of their time together. Royce hadn't realized how much Kelly needed a mother's influence.

As was his habit, Royce read each night. It helped relax him. He expected to have a difficult time falling asleep, but as soon as he turned out the light, he felt himself effortlessly drifting off.

A phone call, especially one in the middle of the night, was never good news. It rang, waking Royce from a deep sleep. He groaned and groped for the receiver, dragging it across the empty pillow at his side.

"Yes?" he demanded.

Silence.

Royce scrambled into a sitting position. Something told him it was Catherine on the other end of the line. Some inner instinct.

"Catherine?" he asked, his heart racing. "Answer me. What's wrong?"

Seven

Catherine felt like an idiot, phoning Royce in the middle of the night. She didn't know what had prompted her to do anything so foolish, nor did she know what she intended to say once he picked up the receiver. As soon as he answered, she realized her folly and was about to disconnect the line when he called her name.

"H-how'd you know it was me?" She pushed the hair off her forehead and drew in soft, catching gasps in an effort to stop the flow of tears that refused to cease.

"It was a good guess," Royce admitted gently. "Now tell me what's wrong."

If only he'd been outraged, instead of caring. She might have been able to avoid telling him, but she needed him so desperately—as desperately as she'd ever needed anyone. "I'm fine, really I am," she lied. "It's just that I'm a little out of sorts and…" She couldn't admit to him she hadn't wept, really down-and-out wept in years, and once the tears had started, it was like a dam bursting over a restraining wall. Nothing she tried to do helped.

"Catherine, love, it's two-thirty in the morning. You wouldn't have phoned if everything was peachy keen."

She swallowed a sob and knew the noise she made sounded as though she were drowning, going underwater for the third and last time. "Thank you."

"For what?"

She gnawed on the corner of her lip and ran a tissue under her nose. "For calling me your love. I…need that right now." She was convinced he had no idea he'd used the affectionate term.

He hesitated, then gently pried again. "Are you going to tell me what's wrong?"

Catherine sat curled up on her sofa, her feet tucked beneath her. The pages of her mother's letter were scattered across the top of her coffee table. She'd moved the picture of her father down from the mantel and set it in front of her as well. For part of the night she'd held it to her breast and rocked to and fro in a frantic effort to hold on to him. The area around her was strewn with used tissues.

"Catherine," Royce repeated. "What's wrong?"

"I…I shouldn't have phoned. I'm sorry…I

was going to hang up, but then you said my name."

"I'll be right over."

"Royce, no…please don't." She couldn't deal with him, not now. In addition, her apartment complex was full of Navy personnel. If anyone were to see Royce coming in or out of her apartment in the early hours of the morning, it could be disastrous.

"Then tell me what's troubling you."

Catherine reached for another tissue. "I got a letter from my mother…" she sobbed. A fresh batch of hot tears coursed down her face, streaking it with glistening trails of pain. Even now, hours after reading the letter, her mother's news had the power to wrench her heart. "You're going to think I'm so stupid to be this upset."

"I won't think anything of the sort."

"She's getting married. I don't expect you to understand…how can you when I don't understand myself…but it's like she's turning her back on my father after all these years. She loved him so much. She deserves to be happy but I can't help thinking…there'll be no one to remember…my dad."

"Just because your mother's marrying doesn't mean she's forgetting your father."

"I've been telling myself that all night, but it just doesn't seem to sink into my heart. I'm happy…for h-her." Catherine sobbed so hard her shoulders shook. "I'm really p-pleased. She's been dating Norman for ten years. It isn't that this is any surprise…I don't even know why I'm crying, but now I can't seem to stop. I feel like such a fool…I'm sorry I woke you. Please go back to sleep and forget I—"

"No," he whispered softly. "There's an old road off Byron Way. Just head north and you can't miss it. I'll meet you there in thirty minutes."

"Royce…" She meant to tell him to forget everything, that she was overreacting, behaving like an insecure child. Instead she found herself asking, "What about Kelly?"

"I'll have a friend come over. If he can't, I'll bring her along. Don't worry." The buzzing noise told her he'd hung up the receiver.

She shouldn't meet him. Catherine told herself that at least a dozen times as she drove down Byron Way. It wasn't fair to Royce to drag him out of bed in the middle of the night to an obscure road just because she couldn't deal with the fact her mother was marrying Norman. Dear, sweet Norman, who'd loved her mother for years and years, who'd patiently waited for her to love him enough to let go of the past.

Catherine managed to hold back the emotion while she struggled to find the road Royce had mentioned, but she felt as unstable as a hundred-year-old prairie farmhouse in a tornado. The first gust of wind and she'd collapse.

Royce was standing outside his car, waiting for her. The moonlight reflected off the hood, illuminating his face, which was creased with anxiety.

Catherine pulled off to the side of the road and turned off her engine. She didn't need a mirror to tell her she looked like hell warmed over, as her mother so often teased. Her eyes were red and swollen, and heaven only knew which direction her hair was pointing.

None of that seemed to matter when Royce walked over to her. He stared down on her as if she were a beauty queen, as if she were the most attractive woman in the world. His world. His eyes wandered over her face, and he raised his hand and caressed her cheek with his fingers.

If he hadn't been so gentle she might have been able to pull it off. She might have been able to convince him she was fine, thank him for his concern and then blithely drive away, no worse for wear. Royce destroyed her plans with his tenderness. He demolished her thin facade with a single look. Tears welled in her eyes, and she placed the tips of her fingers over her mouth in an effort to hold back the wails of grief and anguish that she had yet to fathom.

Royce reached for her then, pulling her into his arms. She went sobbing, banding her arms around his waist. She buried her face in his chest, not wanting him to know how hard she was weeping.

He led her to his Porsche and helped her inside, then joined her, taking her once more into the sanctuary of his arms. Again and again, he stroked the back of her head, again and again he whispered soothing words she couldn't hear over the sound of her own weeping. Again and again, he brushed his chin over the top of her head.

"It's all right," he whispered. "Go ahead and cry."

"I…can't seem to stop. Oh, Royce, I don't understand why I feel like this. I'm…I'm so afraid everyone is going to forget him. And it would be so unfair."

"You aren't going to forget."

"Don't you see?" she sobbed even harder. *"I don't remember anything about him."* Her throat was so thick she couldn't speak for several moments. "I was so young when he went away. Mom tried to help me remember. She told me story after story about all the things we used to do together and how much he loved us. As hard as I try I can't remember a single detail. Nothing."

"But he's alive here," Royce said gently, pressing a hand over her heart, "and that's all that matters."

Catherine wished it were that easy. But her emotions were far more complicated, as complicated as her love for Royce. Being in his arms, drinking in his strength and his comfort, helped to abate the tears.

"Kiss me," she pleaded, craving the healing balm of his love. "Just once and then…I promise I won't bother you again. I'll leave, and you can go back home."

He didn't hesitate. His hands were in her hair, his splayed fingers buried deep, angling her head so that his mouth could sweep down to capture hers the way a circling hawk comes after its prey.

Catherine sighed in appreciation, opening to him. Royce groaned, thrusting his tongue deep into the moist warmth of her mouth. She sighed anew and welcomed the spirals of heat that coiled in her stomach. Her hands gripped his shirt, holding on to him, needing the anchor of his love now more than ever before. The emotion that had been playing havoc with her senses all evening burst wide open and spilled over her like warm, melting honey.

Catherine whimpered.

Royce moaned softly, seeming to experience the same wonder. His hands roved over her back, dragging her forward until their hearts were pressed against each other's, each pounding out a chaotic rhythm of love and need.

When her breasts made contact with his chest, Catherine experienced a sensual hunger she had never known, a need that went beyond the physical. It was as if she were emotionally starved, as if the bleakness of her existence had been laid bare.

Royce's lips claimed hers a second time with an urgency that took her by surprise, his kiss of fierce possession, a deepening urgency, a ferocious hunger neither would be able to tolerate for long.

Royce must have sensed it, too, because he abruptly broke away, his chest heaving with the effort. Catherine longed to protest, but he raised his hand to her face and gently pressed his palm against her heated cheek. Her fingers covered his, and she closed her eyes, savoring this closeness.

When she looked up at him, she found him staring at her. Her eyes didn't waver from his. With unhurried ease, he bent forward and kissed her again, only this time his kiss was slow and tender, as slow and tender as the one before had been untamed and harsh.

"I want to taste you." The heat in his eyes

and in his words caused her to shiver. His hands expertly parted her blouse, and when he discovered she wasn't wearing a bra, his eyes narrowed into blue slits. His hands cupped her breasts and lifted them until they'd formed perfect rounds in his palms. Her nipples had tightened even before he began stroking them with his thumbs. Catherine went still, afraid even to breathe, her eyes half-closed as she dealt with the intense pleasure his hands brought her. His mouth followed, and she rolled her head back and moaned even before his mouth closed over her nipple. With her eyes slammed shut, she arched her back. The impact was so keen, so intense, she longed to cry out.

All too soon his mouth returned to hers and she opened to him, greedily accepting what he was offering. Her hands slid along the curve of his back and up to the thickness of his mussed hair.

Royce's kisses were sweet and warm. Sweet and gentle; too gentle. He broke away completely and rubbed his face against the side of her jaw with a moist foray of nibbling kisses, working his way down her neckline.

"I want to make love to you," he whispered, then quickly amended. "I *need* to make love to you, but damn it all, Catherine, I refuse to do it in the front seat of a car."

With eyes still closed and her heart thundering like a Nebraska storm, she grinned. "Any bed will do."

"You're making this difficult."

"Has it ever been easy for us?"

"No," he growled, his hands continuing to caress her breasts. "You make me feel seventeen all over again."

"It's the car, trust me."

"Maybe." He shifted his weight and groaned, the sound rich and masculine. "I just hope the seamstress who sewed these pants took her job seriously."

Involuntarily, Catherine's gaze dropped to the bulge in his loins. Against her better judgment she trailed her knuckles over it, feeling the heat even through the thickness of his jeans.

The temptation was so powerful that she had to force herself to look away. She sighed, her shoulders lifted several inches with the effort.

Wrapping his arms around her, Royce pulled her toward him, until her back was cushioned by his chest. He leaned forward and slowly rotated his cheek over hers, nuzzling her ear with his nose. "Tell me about your mother."

Catherine grinned, content for the first time since the mail had arrived. "You'd like her. She's wonderfully witty and intelligent. To look at her, you'd never guess she's in her early fifties, almost everyone assumes she's at least ten years younger. The best part is that she's strikingly attractive and doesn't realize it. For the past fifteen years she's lived in San Francisco, and works at the corporate headquarters for this huge importing business. That's where she met Norman. He's a widower, and I swear he fell in love with Mom the minute they met. He's waited ten years for this day, and as much as I love my father, I can't begrudge Mom and Norman any happiness."

"It sounds like mother and daughter are a good deal alike." Royce murmured.

Catherine had to think on that a moment. "Yes, I suppose that's true…I just never thought much about it." Catherine hesitated, then added, "She loved my father."

"Loves," he corrected gently.

"Loves," Catherine agreed softly.

"You're close?"

"Always. She's incredible. If you meet her and still think we're alike, then it would be the greatest compliment anyone could ever give me."

"I think you're incredible," he whispered, playfully nuzzling her neck. His arms were tightly wrapped around her middle, and she felt as though she were in the most secure place in all the world—in Royce's loving arms.

Content, Catherine smiled, folded her arms

over his and closed her eyes. "What are we going to do, Royce?"

She felt the harsh sigh work its way across his chest. It was a question she was sure he'd asked himself a hundred times. One that had hounded them both for weeks, and they were no closer now to a solution than they had been before.

"I wish I knew." It went without saying that if they continued in this vein they were both going to be booted out of the Navy. "I never thought I'd be jealous of my own daughter."

"Of Kelly?" Catherine didn't understand.

"Yes, of Kelly." His grip around her middle tightened. "She, at least, can spend the night with you."

Catherine grinned and nestled back in his arms.

"How do you think I felt learning that you sleep in a little slip of lace that's all see-through on top?"

"She told you that?" Catherine asked, twisting around.

"Yes! Is it true?"

"Yes."

Royce groaned. "You could have lied…I wish you had lied."

"Did she also tell you I sleep on ivory-colored satin sheets?"

"No, she was merciful enough to skip over

that part," he growled in her ear. "Oh, sweet heaven, it feels so good to hold you in my arms. I could get drunk on you."

Catherine was equally content, although she was likely to suffer in the morning. The console was digging into her hip, but it was a small price to pay for the pleasure of being in Royce's arms.

"You're going to be all right now?"

She nodded. "I don't know what came over me. Obviously I have a lot of unresolved feelings for my father."

"Don't get so philosophical. Your mother is letting go of an important part of your lives together. It's only natural for you to feel a certain amount of regret."

There was a lot more than regret in that raging storm of tears that overtook her, but Royce didn't know that. Catherine had yet to fully comprehend the blitz of feelings herself. Her emotions were hopelessly tangled. But it didn't matter, she could face anything or anyone as long as Royce was by her side, as long as the man she loved would hold her tight.

The orders Royce received to conduct an underway inspection aboard the USS *Venture,* a small service craft used by the base, seemed like a godsend. Royce needed time away from Bangor, and from Catherine. The time away was essential to his peace of mind. Three days aboard the *Venture* would help him gain some perspective on what was happening between them.

A hundred times he'd told himself to stay away from her. They were playing with a lit stick of dynamite. The fact they were both doing it with their eyes wide open frustrated him even more.

Royce had done everything he knew to get her out of his mind. He'd ignored her, pretended she didn't exist. When it came to dealing with her at the office, he made her a faceless name and tried to react to her that way. He'd had women under his command before without there ever being so much as a hint of a problem.

The difficulty was it didn't work. Royce couldn't ignore Catherine any more than he could jump over the moon. It was a physical impossibility. He couldn't look at her, even in the most impersonal way, and not hunger for the taste of her. It went without saying that a single taste would never satisfy him, and he knew it. He had to feel her, had to run his hands down the soft curving slopes of her body and experience for himself her ready response to his touch.

Some mornings he walked into the office and with one glance at her he'd been forced to knot his hands at his sides just to keep from reaching for her. The ache would start then and last all day and sometimes long into the night. Was it any wonder his men had come up with a few choice names for him while he was in his present state of mind?

The physical frustration was killing him, and as far as Royce could tell it was going to get a hell of a lot worse before it got better.

Just when Royce was foolish enough to believe he had everything under control, she'd called him, weeping in the middle of the night. If he hadn't been so starved for her, he might have been able to handle the situation differently. But the moment he'd heard her weep, the urge to take her in his arms and comfort her had been overwhelming. Already it was happening. What he swore never would. He arranged for them to meet in some out-of-the-way place where no one was likely to see them.

Royce justified the meeting, remembering how she'd been there for him when Kelly was in the hospital. Helping her deal with the fact her mother was going to remarry was returning the kindness, nothing more.

To further vindicate his actions, he'd convinced himself that he'd have done the same thing for anyone under his command. That might be true, but he doubted that he'd meet them at the end of a long dirt road. Nor would he hold and kiss them the way he did Catherine.

From that night forward, matters had only gotten worse. Royce could feel his control slipping even more than before. Twice he found himself looking for excuses to call her into his office just so he could hear the sound of her voice. It was coming to the point that she was able to maintain protocol much better than he was. A bad sign. A very bad sign.

Kelly wasn't helping matters any. If having to deal with Catherine at the office wasn't bad enough, Kelly talked about her constantly. The kid was crazy about Catherine and had been from the moment they'd met. At first Royce was convinced it was the fingernails, but gradually, in a slow and painful process, he'd come to realize how badly Kelly needed a mother figure. Why she chose Catherine and not Missy's mom or any of the mothers of her friends, Royce had yet to understand. Instead she'd chosen the one woman who was driving Royce slowly out of his mind.

This assignment aboard the *Venture* was exactly what he needed. Time away.

Royce was packing his bag when Kelly wandered into the bedroom. She plopped herself down on the edge of the mattress and sighed as though she were being abandoned.

"How long are you going to be gone?"

Royce had told her no less than four times, but she continued to ask anyway. "Three days."

Kelly had wanted to spend the time with Catherine, but it made more sense for her to stay with Missy's family since the two girls were in the same class at school. Kelly hadn't been overly thrilled, but she hadn't argued. At least not any more than she usually did.

"When you get back, can we go for pizza?"

"Sure," Royce agreed, glancing up long enough to smile at her. He didn't know why she asked, they always went out to eat when he arrived home from an assignment. It had become tradition.

The phone rang, and Kelly leaped off the bed as though she'd received an electric shock. Even though Royce was less than three feet away, she screamed at the top of her voice, "I'll get it."

Inserting his little finger in his ear, Royce cleared the passageway and resumed packing.

Kelly appeared a minute or so later. "It's for you," she said, sounding disappointed. "It sounds like Captain Garland."

Royce nodded. "Tell him I'll be right there."

Royce finished tucking his socks into the corner of the bag and then went down the hallway. Kelly handed him the phone and leaned against the wall and waited until he'd finished.

The conversation with his commanding officer didn't last more than a couple of minutes. But each one of those minutes might as well have been a lifetime as far as Royce was concerned. What was it that was said about the best laid plans? He didn't know. Hell he didn't know much of anything anymore.

"What's wrong?" Kelly asked once he'd replaced the receiver.

"How do you know that anything's wrong?"

"Because you've got that look again."

Royce didn't know what she was talking about, and frankly he wasn't sure he cared to.

His daughter, however, was bent on telling him. "It's hard to explain," Kelly added on a thoughtful note. "It's a look you get when you're mad and trying not to show it. Your ears get red on the top and your mouth goes like this." She scrunched up her lips like an old prune.

"I never look like that," Royce told her with more than a suggestion of impatience.

"If you say so."

At least she was smart enough to know when not to argue with him, look or not. For that, Royce could be grateful.

He was halfway back to his room when he decided he might as well let Kelly know. "Catherine's coming along with me."

"She is?" Kelly sounded downright thrilled. "How come?"

"There's been a complaint of sexual harassment on board the *Venture* that she's going to investigate. Captain Garland felt it made sense to send us both up at the same time."

"He is the captain," the ten-year-old said with an air of great wisdom.

If Kelly thought to comfort him, she'd failed. Miserably.

It wasn't until they were both aboard the plane that Royce spoke to Catherine. She was sitting in the seat next to him, but he'd done his damnedest to ignore her. Not that it had done any good. Not that it ever did, but he liked to pretend otherwise.

"How'd you arrange this?" he demanded, his voice dripping with sarcasm.

"I didn't," she said, without looking up from the report she was reviewing. "I was ordered to accompany you." She made it sound as though she'd rather be anyplace else than sitting next to him.

Royce looked out the window, unexpectedly amused by her tart reply. Apparently she wasn't any more pleased about this than he was. Well that was par for the course as far as their relationship went.

"If it's any comfort to you I'll be away soon enough." There was a militant strain in her voice that challenged him.

Catherine was going away? It wasn't any comfort, in fact it was cause for alarm. "What do you mean?"

"I'll be attending my mother's wedding."

"I see." Royce hadn't seen the request yet, but he knew there wouldn't be any problem in granting her leave.

"Unfortunately that isn't going to help," he growled. The need to touch her, even in the smallest way, was so strong Royce couldn't fight it anymore. He moved his leg just enough so his calf could brush against hers. He nearly sighed in relief. Her skin felt silky and smooth, so smooth.

The movement, almost invisible to anyone else quickly captured Catherine's attention. She jerked her head up and frowned at him.

"Royce," she breathed, "what are you doing?"

"Looking for a way to get booted out of the Navy it seems."

She yanked her leg away, expelled a shuddering sigh and returned to the report she was reading. But Royce noticed that her hands were trembling.

Who was he kidding? If anyone was shaking it was he. It started that first afternoon on the track when Catherine had refused to stop running, and it hadn't lessened since.

Royce laid back his head and closed his eyes. He needed to think. He'd come a hair's space from making love to her in the front seat of a car. He was meeting her on dirt roads. Now he was reduced to trying to feel her up while on a military transport.

He was in bad shape. Worse than he thought. Only a desperate man would have pulled that trick. Which said a lot about his mental condition. This assignment was going to be a hell of a lot more difficult than he'd imagined.

That thought proved to be more prophetic than Royce ever dreamed. The first day into the inspection he was so angry he walked around in a red haze. He wasn't civil to be around. It was so bad, he didn't even like himself. And for what reason? Because Lieutenant Commander Masterson had taken an instant liking to Catherine. The man had made his interest in her known from the moment they'd stepped on board the *Venture.*

Royce was making notes when he inadvertently happened upon Masterson talking to Catherine in the narrow hallway. He didn't like the familiar way in which the young lieutenant commander was leaning toward her. Nor did he appreciate the way the other man was looking at her as though he couldn't wait to get her into his bed.

"Are you finished with your report?" he demanded of Catherine.

"Not yet." She looked surprised that he'd even ask since the account of the complaint wasn't due for several days after their return.

"Then I suggest you start work on it."

"Yes, sir." She started to walk past him when Royce turned on Masterson, his eyes narrowed into dark slits. He couldn't remember a time he'd wanted to take a man down more.

"Problems?" Masterson asked innocently enough.

"This isn't the Love Boat, Lieutenant Commander," Royce said as scathingly as he could. "Captain Garland didn't ask Lieutenant Commander Fredrickson to accompany me for your entertainment."

The other man's eyes widened at the verbal attack.

"I suggest you keep your hands to yourself."

"But he didn't…" Catherine intervened, until Royce turned on her, making sure his eyes were hard enough to effectively silence her. She had no business speaking to him. No business defending Masterson, and that infuriated him even more.

"You're both dismissed," he said harshly, and waited until they'd retreated in opposite directions.

In the next twenty-four hours, Royce didn't say more than a handful of words to Catherine. In fact he was avoiding her. She was avoiding him, too. Like the plague. But then so was everyone else—not that he blamed them.

Royce was tired. Mentally and physically. But keyed up at the same time. Before heading off to bed, he decided to stop off in the galley for a cup of coffee. Caffeine sometimes helped to relax him.

He apparently wasn't the only one who needed something that night. Catherine sat at the table and glanced up when he appeared. She looked startled, as though she'd been caught doing something illegal.

"I'll leave," she said, slowly coming to her feet.

"No, stay," he returned crisply, walking over to the coffeepot.

"Is that an order?"

He had to think about it a moment. "Yes."

Her hands cupped the mug. Her gaze was centered on the steaming liquid as though something were about to leap out.

Royce poured himself a cup and sat down across from her. He didn't say anything for several moments, then decided now was as good a time as any to speak his mind. As bad a time as any for that matter. At least they were alone.

"I don't like the way Masterson's been looking at you," he admitted, frowning as he did so.

Catherine's head flew up so fast it was a wonder she didn't injure her neck.

"Lieutenant Commander Masterson?"

"Yes," he said roughly. He knew he sounded possessive, but he couldn't help himself. It had been eating at him from the moment they'd arrived. Mark Masterson had made a fool of himself over Catherine. Everyone had noticed. Certainly Catherine must have. Royce had even heard a couple of the men talking about the way Masterson had an eye for the ladies.

"You mean to say you've been acting like a…a…" Apparently she couldn't think of anything bad enough. "Like a moron because you're…jealous?" Her words were issued vehemently in a whisper.

"I have not been acting like a moron," he denied hotly, in the same low tones she used. "I have eyes."

"And what would you like me to do about it?"

Her words took Royce by surprise. He expected her to deny it, claim it was all in his head. He even thought she'd call him a fool for saying it. Okay, she'd called him a moron. That was close. What he hadn't anticipated was her acceptance of the problem.

"Well?" she demanded.

"What do I expect you to do about it?" he repeated. The answer came to him then, as profoundly as anything he'd ever felt. It was all so simple. It was all so complicated.

"Marrying me would settle it."

Eight

"You don't mean that," Catherine whispered, confident Royce's proposal had been prompted by a fit of jealous rage. She would never have guessed that Royce would be so insecure.

Sadly, Catherine couldn't deny that the lieutenant commander had gone out of his way to let her know he was interested. In what, she wasn't entirely sure. Mark Masterson had been more than attentive from the moment she and Royce had landed aboard the *Venture*. He hadn't done anything offensive, and under other circumstances Catherine might have been flattered. Certainly she'd done nothing to encourage his attention.

"The hell I don't mean it," Royce countered sharply, impatiently. His face was scowled in an intimidating frown that pleated his brow in thick folds.

"You don't need to shout at me."

Royce lowered his voice several decibels. "I am not yelling. Will you or won't you marry me?"

"I can't," she felt obliged to remind him. She was under his command, which was something he'd conveniently forgotten. Any relationship, other than one that involved Navy business, was strictly prohibited. He knew it. She knew it. But for pride's sake Royce had chosen to overlook the fact.

Slowly Royce stiffened, as though anticipating a body blow, as if he were unsure of her and her love. "Would you marry me if it were possible?"

"Probably."

"Probably," he repeated, his eyes rounding. It was as though she'd issued him the greatest insult of his life.

"Yes, probably," she returned just as heatedly. "If the proposal weren't issued on the tail end of a fit of jealousy and...and if I were convinced to the soles of my feet that you loved me."

"I love you." This, too, was discharged as if he were tallying points in a heated debate. "So what's your answer? Yes or no?"

"Just like that?"

"Just like that." He made it sound as if there shouldn't be anything to consider, as if he were asking her out to dinner, instead of a complicated relationship that would involve disrupting both their lives, and Kelly's, not to mention their careers.

"Why?" she charged, "so I can inform Masterson I'm an engaged woman?"

"Yes," Royce confirmed without pause. His hands were cupped around his coffee with enough force to shatter the ceramic mug.

"Then thanks, but no thanks." Battling righteousness, Catherine stood abruptly, prepared to leave the room. How dare Royce offer her marriage in an effort to salvage his precious male pride. The only reason he'd even suggested it was out of concern she might be attracted to Mark Masterson. The ironic part of all this was that Royce had only recently tried to arrange a date for her with Dan Parker. In the space of a few short weeks, he'd gone from one extreme to another. Catherine didn't know what to expect next.

"What do you mean *no thanks?*" Royce demanded, leaping to his feet with enough force to topple his chair. Somehow he managed to catch it before it crashed to the floor.

"I don't know how much plainer I can make it, Commander. The answer is *no.*"

He looked positively stunned, as if she'd stepped forward and thrust a sword between his ribs. He'd been so sure of himself, so damned arrogant, as if it were a foregone conclusion she'd accept his offer of marriage without even needing to think it over. It hurt her pride that he'd proposed in such a callous manner with a complete lack of tenderness or romance.

"If and when I marry," she felt obliged to explain, "it will be to a man who doesn't behave like a jealous idiot. Someone who demonstrates his love with a tad more finesse than to shout out a proposal in a ship's galley because he's afraid someone else might do it before he gets the chance. Now, if you'll excuse me, I'm going to my stateroom." With that she stalked away.

To her dismay, Royce followed her down the long, narrow passageway. He was so close behind her, Catherine feared he was about to step on her heels. She hadn't a clue what he intended to say or how far he planned on following her. Outside her quarters, she vaulted around and confronted him.

"You wanted to say something?" she demanded.

"You're damn right I do."

In all the time Catherine had worked with Royce, she'd never seen him like this, as though he'd been driven to the very limit of his endur-
ce.

ht I suggest we discuss this at a more ap-
e, Commander," she said, her voice

bordering on impertinence. She'd gone about as far as she dared with Royce, but she couldn't, wouldn't allow him to pull rank on her with an issue that was strictly personal.

"No, you may not." After looking both ways, he opened the door to her quarters and gently pushed her inside.

"What the hell do you think you're doing?" she insisted.

Royce didn't answer her. Instead he backed her against the bulkhead. His large, muscular hands settled over her shoulders, dragging her against him. Her struggles were of little good against his superior strength. Arching her back was a mistake as well. It only served to bring the lower half of her body in intimate contact with his. She was about to cry out in protest when his mouth smothered hers, his lips ruthlessly grinding over hers. Immediately his tongue was there, flickering softly over her lips, coaxing them open. Catherine fought him, fought herself for as long as she could hold out, which was a humiliatingly short time. With tears crowding her eyes, she parted her lips, welcoming the intrusion of his tongue, meeting it with her own. Royce groaned when she opened to him, and her moans of outrage and anger quickly became soft cries of bliss.

"Royce!" she cried, jerking her

side. Her shoulders heaved with the effort. "Are you crazy?"

"Yes." He didn't bother to deny it. Gradually he released her and took a moment to compose himself. "I have no excuse for this. Forgive me, Catherine." No sooner had the words been spoken when he was gone, leaving her to wonder if anyone had witnessed him coming out of her quarters.

Marilyn Fredrickson moved around the kitchen, her silk robe knotted at her trim waist. As Catherine watched her mother, she was struck anew by what an attractive woman Marilyn was. Petite, beautiful and intuitive, far more intuitive than Catherine remembered.

Marilyn brought the coffeepot around the kitchen counter where Catherine was sitting on a high stool. She, too, was dressed in her housecoat, her hair mussed. Catherine loved her mother's kitchen more every time she came to visit. It was painted a light shade of cheery yellow, with bright sunlight spilling in from the three skylights overhead. The counters were white with a huge wicker basket of dried flowers decorating the corner.

"So are you going to tell me about him?" Marilyn asked, slipping onto the stool next to Catherine.

She hadn't mentioned a word about Royce. Her flight from Seattle had landed late the night before. Her mother and Norman had picked her up at the airport, and they'd driven directly to the condo in San Francisco's refurbished Marina District. Catherine and her mother had stayed up half the night, but all the talk had evolved around her mother and Norman. Not once had Catherine mentioned Royce.

"About who?" she asked innocently, not sure even now she could talk about him.

Her mother's smile was chiding. She raised the coffee cup to her lips and took a sip, then sighed. "I remember the day Norman asked me to marry him. It wasn't the first time, mind you, but he hadn't pressed me in more than a year. I asked for more time, the way I always do. Ever the gentleman, Norman accepted that, but then he said something he never had before. He said he loved me, and always would, but he explained that a man only has so much patience. He was tired of living his life alone, tired of dreaming of having me for his wife one day. Then he asked me if I truly loved him."

"You do." Catherine already knew the answer to that.

"Of course I do, I have for years." Marilyn paused once more for another drink of her coffee, which gave her time to compose her thoughts, it seemed. "That night as I was getting ready for bed, I stood in front of the bathroom mirror to remove my makeup. As I stared at my reflection I realized there was a certain look about me, a certain…I hesitate to use this word, readiness."

"Readiness," Catherine repeated.

"Yes. Right then and there I realized what a fool I'd been to wait so many years to marry Norman. The time was right to accept his proposal, it had been right for a good long while, only I hadn't realized it. I couldn't even wait until morning, I phoned him right then." Her lips quivered gently with a smile. "I took one look at you this morning, Catherine, and there's a certain look about you not unlike the one I saw in myself."

"Readiness?" Catherine joked.

"No, not that. You have the look of a woman in love, but one who doesn't know what she's going to do. Do you want to talk about it?"

"I…don't know." Catherine had left for California shortly after her return to Bangor from the *Venture*. She hadn't seen Royce in three days prior to her departure, nor had she spoken to him since that one horrible night aboard the Navy vessel. Every time she thought about Royce's marriage proposal, she was forced to wade through a mine field of negative emotions, each one threatening to explode in her face.

Her mother was watching her closely, and Catherine realized she owed her some explanation. "There are difficulties."

"Is he married?"

Her startled gaze flew to Marilyn's. "Nothing that drastic."

"I take it he's in the Navy?"

Catherine nodded. "That's the problem. He's the executive officer, my boss."

Her mother knew what that meant without Catherine needing to explain it. The dark brown eyes narrowed slightly. "Oh, Catherine, sweetie, you do like to live dangerously, don't you?"

"It wasn't like I planned to fall in love with him," she cried, defending herself. No one in their right mind would purposely put themselves through this torment.

"Does he return your feelings?"

"I think so." After the night he'd met her on the dirt road, Catherine was convinced she'd never question the way he felt about her. Then he'd pulled that stunt aboard the *Venture* and she was left sinking with doubts.

"You think so?" Marilyn repeated slowly, thoughtfully. It seemed her mother was incredulous that Catherine wouldn't know something this important.

"He loves me," she amended.

"He just has a difficult time showing it?"

"Exactly." Catherine replayed the latest incident and how he'd followed her into her cabin. It had been a foolish risk that might have cost them both dearly.

"I take it you rejected his marriage proposal?"

"Of course I did. He asked for all the wrong reasons."

"But if he asked for all the right ones, what would you have said?"

"Honest to God truth?" Catherine asked.

"Honest to God truth."

"Yes. In a heartbeat. Oh, Mom, I'm so crazy about this guy—I don't know what's right anymore. I never dreamed I'd defy Navy regulations. It's simply not done. Yet here we are so crazy in love we're acting like complete idiots, risking our careers and our reputations and everything else I always thought was so important...I still think is important.

"I know Royce was upset that I'd been assigned to accompany him on the *Venture*. He'd wanted this time apart to gain some perspective about us and our relationship. At least I assume that was what he intended. Then I was ordered to accompany him, and it made everything much worse. Everything seems to be working against us."

"What's going to happen when you return?"

Catherine sighed and slowly shook her head. "I wish I knew."

"Royce...that's his name?" At Catherine's nod, Marilyn continued. "He'll have the time you seem to think he needs."

"But, Mom," Catherine said, feeling more miserable than ever, "if he does decide it would be best for us to marry, it won't help matters any. We'd both continue to paddle in the same leaky boat as before."

"But if you marry Royce, won't you give up the Navy?"

"No," she cried vehemently. "Why should I? I love the military. I'm not about to relinquish an eleven-year investment just because I happen to fall in love. And getting out of the Navy isn't all that easy, either. It takes up to a year, unless I were to find myself pregnant."

Marilyn's eyebrows shot toward her hairline.

"Oh, Mother, honestly. There's no possibility."

"I'm sorry, sweetie, it's just that I'd love to have grandchildren someday."

"I'll do my best—someday."

Marilyn rested her elbows on the counter and released an elongated sigh. "I hadn't realized getting out of the Navy would be such a hassle."

"I'm not leaving the Navy," Catherine reinforced.

"So what's going to happen?"

Her mother asked the question as though Catherine kept a crystal ball in her pocket and consulted it regularly. "The only thing either one of us can do is put in a request for a transfer."

"But you just moved to Bangor from Hawaii."

"I know. It isn't likely the Navy will look favorably upon shipping me elsewhere anytime soon."

"What about Royce? Can he put in a request?"

Catherine bit into her lower lip. It was a thought she'd entertained often, although she'd never spoken to Royce about it. "Yes, but I don't know that he will. He's been stationed at Bangor for several years now, and he'd hate to uproot Kelly. It's the only home she's ever known. Of course there's always the chance he'd be reassigned to one of the other commands in the Puget Sound area. We can hope, of course."

"Kelly? Who's Kelly?"

Catherine doubted that her mother had heard anything beyond the point that she'd mentioned Royce's daughter's name. "His daughter. She's ten and oh, Mom, she is such a delight. We get along so well. She's just at the age where she's discovering what it means to be a girl. It all started with me painting her fingernails when she was hurt in an accident. We've gotten so close. The last time we met, Kelly wanted her hair cut, so I took her to a salon and stood over the hairdresser like an old mother hen. When she'd finished, Kelly looked so cute."

"You're spending a lot of time with her, I take it?"

"As much as I can," Catherine said, and hesitated. "You're wearing that worried look again."

"I can't help it," Marilyn murmured. "I don't want to see you get hurt."

"I won't," Catherine assured her with more confidence than she was feeling. "Now quit being such a worrywart. This is your wedding day, and I certainly don't want you looking all serious and somber fretting about me." Catherine took a sip of her coffee and glanced at her watch. "Oh, my goodness," she said, sliding off the stool. "Look at the time! We've got to get ready, or you'll be late for your own wedding. Norman will never forgive me."

The wedding was lovely. Her mother made a radiant bride, Catherine mused during the plane trip on the way back to Seattle. Norman had never looked more distinguished or handsome. The two, backed with long years of steady friendship, were the ideal couple. Catherine had heard several people say as much as she wandered through the reception, making sure everyone had what they needed. Norman had insisted the affair be catered, but Catherine had made busywork in an effort to keep herself absorbed. If she'd sat back and relaxed, there might have been time to think about the young, handsome man in the photograph that rested on her fireplace mantel. The father she'd never known.

It was ironic that Catherine would be better acquainted with her new stepfather than the man who'd given her life.

When it came time for her mother and Norman to exchange their vows, Catherine had felt a sudden rush of emotion crowd her eyes. A tear or two did manage to slip down her cheek as she stood beside her mother, clenching a floral bouquet. If anyone noticed, and Catherine prayed they didn't, she sincerely hoped they assumed it was a tear of shared happiness.

Catherine *was* happy for her mother and Norman. Even more so now that she'd experienced these few days with them. It was almost comical watching the two. They were like young lovers, so involved with each other the rest of the world didn't seem to exist.

In many ways Catherine was envious. Her love for Royce was so much more complicated. As the Boeing 737 cut a wide path through the thick layer of clouds, Catherine couldn't help wondering what kind of reception Royce would have for her upon her return. Would he be pleased she was back? Would his eyes search hers out so she'd know how much he'd missed her? Would he find an excuse to be alone with her? Or would the brick facade he so often carried be tightly locked in place? So secure he'd look right through her and reveal little of what he was thinking and none of what he was feeling.

Catherine was exhausted when the plane landed at Sea-Tac. When she walked off the jetway into the airport terminal, she found her gaze scanning the crowds, hoping that Royce would be there waiting for her.

He wasn't.

It was ridiculous to expect him. As far as she knew, he wasn't even aware of her flight schedule. Then why, she asked herself, did she experience this heavy letdown?

"You're an idiot," she whispered as she walked down the concourse to the baggage claim area.

Again she reminded herself what a fool she was when she unlocked her apartment door over an hour later, after she'd picked Sambo up from the neighbor's. To her disappointment, there wasn't anything on her answering machine from Royce, either. Kelly had left two messages. The first call was to tell Catherine that her story about the Princess and the Dragon had been chosen by her teachers for the Young Authors Program. Kelly was so excited and had been talking so fast it was difficult to understand her. The second message had been made that afternoon, Catherine decided, and the purpose was to tell her Kelly missed her and wished she'd hurry back soon.

Catherine toyed with the idea of phoning the ten-year-old, then noted the time and realized Royce's daughter was probably already asleep for the night. It was unlikely that he'd appreciate the intrusion.

Nevertheless, she couldn't give up the idea. Five minutes later, against her better judgment, she found herself reaching for the phone.

It was Royce who answered. His voice was as rich and masculine as ever, and just hearing it sent goose bumps up her spine.

"It's Catherine," she said, managing to keep any emotion out of her voice, "I'm calling for Kelly."

He hesitated, as though she'd caught him off guard. "She went to bed about half an hour ago."

The tension crackled over the telephone wire like static electricity. "Will you tell her I phoned?"

"Of course."

Catherine closed her eyes against the lack of sentiment in his voice. It was as if he were speaking to a casual acquaintance and not the woman he'd once claimed he loved. Once, only once, and then it had come as part of a jealous rage.

"I...I won't keep you then," she announced stiffly.

"You aren't keeping me from anything more than television." His control had slipped just a little, as if he were reluctant to disconnect the line. For that, at least, Catherine could be grateful.

"How was the wedding?" he asked, as though looking for ways to make polite conversation.

"Beautiful," she told him, meaning it.

"How were you?"

He didn't need to explain the question. He was asking how she'd dealt with the emotions she'd had so much trouble accepting when she'd first learned her mother intended to marry Norman.

Involuntarily, Catherine's gaze drifted to her fireplace mantel. "Fine," she whispered. She'd dealt with it splendidly, far better than she'd expected. "Mom made a beautiful bride." Once more there was a noticeable silence. He'd done his part, now it was her turn. "How did everything go at the office?"

"There weren't any problems."

"Good," she whispered. "I'll be back in the morning."

"So I understand."

Say something, Catherine pleaded silently. *Let me know what you're feeling. Tell me you missed me as dreadfully as I missed you. Tell me you regret that we parted without settling our differences.*

Nothing. The line went so quiet that for a moment all Catherine could hear was the sound of her own breathing.

"I'll see you in the morning," she said, when it became apparent Royce had no intention of continuing the stilted conversation.

"Right...in the morning." How clipped he sounded, how eager to be rid of her, but all changed abruptly when he said, "Good night, Catherine."

There was such hunger in those few words, such longing. "Good night," she responded softly.

She pressed the receiver more closely to her ear when she heard him call her name.

"Yes," she said, trying hard to disguise the eagerness in her voice. She sounded like a silly schoolgirl and couldn't have cared less.

"About Mark Masterson."

"Yes?" Her eyes drifted closed, ready to savor his words of apology, ready to apologize herself, anything that would dislodge this ten-foot wall between them. This wall of pride and pain.

"He phoned for you while you were away." Royce's voice hardened until each word fell like a chip of concrete against a hammer.

"Lieutenant Commander Masterson?" Catherine had trouble believing it. She'd done everything possible to discourage the *Venture*'s officer. Catherine couldn't understand why Mark, who had recently gone through a divorce, would turn to her.

"He left a number where you can get in touch with him."

"I have no intention of contacting him," she confirmed, in case Royce suspected she was even remotely interested in the other man.

"What you do or don't do is none of my concern." The hard note in his voice progressed to a savage undertone. "You're free to do as you wish."

"Do you honestly want me to date him?" she challenged, losing patience with Royce.

"What I want isn't a concern here. Masterson left a message for you. Why he chose to contact me to give it to you is anyone's guess. Apparently he's going to be in Bangor sometime soon.

Heaven only knows now ... ...
he did, and he told me to let you know he'll be
looking for you."

"What's that supposed to mean?" Catherine
demanded.

"You can put your own connotation on it because I assure you I don't have a clue."

"I'll bet you don't," Catherine muttered.

"I beg your pardon."

"You heard me, Royce Nyland." The tension
between them was stretched beyond the breaking point.

"Listen, Catherine, if you're waiting for me
to tell you you're free to date Masterson, then
you've got it. Feel free. There's nothing between
us."

Catherine was so hurt and angry, she started
to shake. "Is that a fact? Well, I must admit
I find that interesting. One minute you're demanding I marry you, and in the next you're
practically ordering me to date another man."
She was so upset, she could feel her anger overwhelming her good sense. Sucking in a giant
breath, she forced herself to stop before she said
something she'd regret. "The dirt road off Byron
Way," she said, as calmly as she could manage.
"Meet me there in half an hour."

She didn't wait for him to confirm or deny his
being there, but replaced the receiver.

...when the
...g it, she reached
for her coat and purse and walked out of her
apartment.

Forty minutes later, Catherine was standing
outside her car, her hands stuffed in the pockets of her jacket, searching the night for Royce's
headlights. She'd just about given up hope when
she saw his car come barreling down the road.
At least she assumed it was Royce.

He turned off the engine and leaped out of the
car and stood there. For all his rush, he didn't
seem to have a thing to say.

For that matter, Catherine didn't, either. They
stood staring at each other, the moonlight cas-
cading over them like a golden waterfall, splashing light on either side of them.

He looked dreadful, as though he hadn't slept
in days. His face was stern and harsh, as aus-
tere as she'd ever seen it. Her gaze slid to his. It
seemed for a moment that he wanted to avoid
looking at her, but apparently something com-
pelled him to meet her gaze, but he did so reluctantly. Catherine gasped softly at the way
his deep, cobalt-blue eyes plunged into hers as
though he would have drowned just looking at
her.

"Oh, Royce," she whispered, stepping toward
him, stretching out her arms. Her heart was

so full of love she would cry if he didn't hold her soon.

He met her halfway, wrapping his arms around her waist and lifting her off the ground. With a growl, his mouth met hers in a frenzy of need and desire. They were so starved for each other that an eternity passed before either of them stopped to breathe.

Royce buried his face in the curve of her neck. "I'm sorry, so sorry," he chanted. "I've never been so insanely jealous in my life. I don't know how to deal with it. I've behaved like a fool."

Catherine's hands framed his face. "Just be quiet and kiss me," she ordered ruggedly against his lips. She slipped her tongue forward to meet his, not giving him the opportunity to argue if that had ever been his intention.

If Royce was holding back anything in reserve, he gave it to her then. With a deep-throated moan, he tightened his arms around her, flattening her breasts to his chest. Catherine could feel every part of him, every fiber of his military issue coat, every button, every crease. The kiss was the most primitive they'd shared. The most punishing. Catherine opened to him, and his tongue met hers.

She coiled her arms around his neck and slid down his front. Apparently she became too heavy for him because he lowered her feet to the frozen ground. His hand ran down the length of her spine and then intimately over the curve of her hip. He continued to slide his hands up and down her sides as though he couldn't get enough of her, as though he couldn't believe even now that she was his.

Catherine felt as though the whole world was spinning. It didn't matter. Nothing did as long as she was in his arms.

In the middle of the sweetest, hottest, most intimate kiss of her life, Royce reluctantly tore his mouth away from her. She was gratified to note that his breathing was as labored as her own.

"This doesn't settle anything," he whispered, his breath mingling with hers. His eyes remained closed as though he didn't possess the strength to refuse her anything.

"You're right," she whispered, "but it sure as hell helps." With that she directed his mouth back to her own.

Nine

"I need to get back. I left Kelly at the neighbor's," Royce whispered close to Catherine's ear. They were snuggled up in the front seat of Royce's car, her back against his chest with Royce's arms draped around her. They'd spent the last hour just this way, savoring these stolen moments, not wanting to part for fear of how long it would be before they'd have the chance to hold each other again.

"I need to get back, too," Catherine admitted reluctantly, but neither of them seemed in any hurry to leave.

"One last kiss?" Royce suggested, while spreading nibbling kisses down the side of her ivory neck, pausing now and again to swirl the moist tip of his tongue around her earlobe.

"You wanted a single kiss a half hour ago," she reminded him in a low whisper, "and the next thing I know my bra is missing and you're cursing because you can't find the zipper in my pants."

"That was your fault."

"Mine?" Catherine was indignant. He'd been all over her. They'd been all over each other, so hungry with need it was a gnawing ache in the pit of her stomach still. If it hadn't been for the gearshift, Catherine was convinced they'd have made love several times over by now.

"Yes, your fault," Royce repeated huskily. "If you didn't have such beautiful, tempting breasts." His hands slid up from her midriff to rest against the undersides of her fullness. His hands were close enough to reignite the achy, hollow feeling within her. Her breath escaped in a trickle as his thumbs lazily grazed her throbbing nipples.

"All right," she agreed softly. "Just one kiss." She arched her back and strained upward until her mouth unerringly found his.

Royce claimed her lips roughly, reeling her senses into oblivion. As his mouth worked over hers, his hands roved under her sweater after what seemed like an excruciating delay. Catherine moaned at the sheer wonder of his touch. Royce's tongue breached the barrier of her lips, probing, promising, as his hands caressed the weighted fullness of her breasts, kneading the heated flesh.

Soon Catherine was panting with primitive needs that curled deep inside her. "We're steaming up the windows again," she told him, knowing full well it was their moans and sighs as much as their breaths that were misting the car windows. It was becoming increasingly difficult to rein in their desires, and each time they were together, it became more of a strain, more of a struggle. Catherine had never felt more wanton. Never more wanting.

"The windows are the least of our problems," Royce said in a husky murmur.

She threaded her fingers through his hair and arched upwards, loving him so much she felt drunk with the emotion.

Royce lifted his weight, but his knee slammed hard against the gearshift. He cursed under his breath and rubbed the injured part of his leg. "I'm getting too old for this," he complained.

"We're both too old for this."

"I'm pleased you agree." His hands were at the band of her wool slacks. His touch was warm, and his lips, against the underside of her chin, were decidedly hot. A fluttery sensation rippled over her skin as he slipped the button at the side of her hip free and eased the zipper downward. The sound buzzed in the close confines of the car like a roaring chain saw. Catherine's heart was pounding just as loudly.

* * *

Royce was convinced there was a limit to how much sexual frustration one man could endure. He'd reached it the night before with Catherine in the front seat of his car. *The front seat of his car.* The thought was a sobering one. A man who'd reached the age of thirty-seven shouldn't be attempting to make love in a car seat. There was something ideologically wrong with that.

Only the physical restrictions had prevented him from taking Catherine. If he'd possessed any talent as a contortionist he might have been able to manage it, but he was long past the age of attempting acrobatics.

Royce, however, promised himself he'd never buy a two-seater vehicle again. Never. No matter how sporty looking it was.

That thought was sobering as well. Everything he'd predicted about his and Catherine's relationship was coming to pass. Everything he'd feared. They were already meeting in out-of-the-way places. The sad fact was, Royce knew he wouldn't be able to handle any more sessions like the one they'd recently shared.

The next step was the hotel room. He'd been ready for one the night before. He'd been so incredibly hot for Catherine, he hadn't given a thought to propriety. If the circumstances had been somewhat different he would have driven Catherine to the nearest hotel and damned the consequences. He'd needed her, had wanted her that desperately.

He hadn't, of course, and consequently he'd been trying to forget about his unspent passion for the past twelve hours, with little success.

Once they'd gotten past the physical aspect of their need, or as near to satisfying it as was possible, they'd held each other for another hour and talked.

Royce was amazed that they could find so much to talk about and not mention the one thing that was on both their minds.

What the hell were they going to do?

Royce didn't know. Catherine apparently didn't, either.

Sitting back from his desk, Royce rolled a pen between his palms as he pondered the situation between him and Catherine for the hundredth time that day.

The office was unusually quiet. Everyone had gone home for the day, which was just as well. Catherine was due back from a court session anytime. Royce had left word for her to come directly to his office.

He was anxious to see her. When the hell wasn't he anxious to see her, he asked himself caustically.

It was her eyes, he decided. She had the darkest, most expressive eyes of any woman he'd ever met. They were wistful eyes, that clearly spelled out her thoughts.

And, if he could read her thoughts, then surely everyone else could, too.

How were they supposed to combat that? Royce knotted his hands into tight fists of frustration. He wasn't any closer to finding a solution now than he had been weeks earlier when the problem first presented itself.

Catherine's eyes were also the most provocative ones he'd ever encountered. She'd look up and smile at him, that secret, sexy smile, and then her eyes would meet his, and Royce swore she told him everything she hungered for in a single look. Apparently she found her own thoughts embarrassing because she'd start to blush and her eyelashes would flutter and she'd quickly glance away. It was all Royce could do not to make love to her then and there.

If there was anything to be grateful for, Royce realized, it was that she'd yet to give him that look while in the office.

The polite knock at his door cut into Royce's thoughts. He recognized the short, abrupt rap as Catherine's.

"Come in," he called out.

She stepped inside the room and automatically closed the door. "You wanted to see me?"

He noted that her gaze just missed meeting his. Royce didn't know whether to be grateful or not. Matters being as they were, he probably should be.

"Sit down, Lieutenant Commander."

Her gaze briefly skidded to his, and he knew she was attempting to read his mood. Generally he didn't refer to her by her rank unless he was attempting to put some distance between them.

Catherine pulled out the chair and sat down.

Royce had spent a good portion of the day struggling with the problems between them, trying to formulate a solution. He wasn't any closer now than the time he first accepted his feelings for Catherine weren't going to go away. It was either deal with them now or later. And later could prove risky to their careers.

"How are you?" he asked, not knowing exactly where to start. Asking about her health was a stall tactic and not one he employed often.

"Fine. And you?"

"Well." As well as could be expected under the circumstances, he amended mentally.

Her fingers were clenched tightly in her lap, and she flexed and unflexed them a couple of times in nervous anticipation. Royce wondered briefly why she should be so ill at ease. Then he realized that the only times he'd ever called her into his office it had been to reprimand her for one thing or another.

"Relax, Catherine," he said, lowering his own guard. "We need to talk, and this seemed to be the safest place." And the most dangerous, but Royce felt it essential to clear the air between them. To do it without the physical temptations clouding their judgments as had so often happened in the past. The only other place he could think to speak to her was the jogging track, and he couldn't be assured of privacy there.

"I was thinking we needed to talk, too," she said, her voice little more than a faint murmur.

"Then it looks like we've come to similar conclusions."

Her beautiful, expressive eyes shot to his, and he could read her alarm as clearly as if she'd spelled it out.

"W-what have you decided?" she asked outright.

If only Royce could reach a conclusion. "I haven't," he admitted with heavy reluctance. "I thought I'd have a chance to sort everything out while I was aboard the *Venture*. When that didn't pan out, I was hoping to have some time to think while you were with your mother." He'd soon discovered, however, that he missed her too much to be objective.

"I thought I might be able to do some thinking myself," Catherine interjected softly.

"And did you come to any decisions?"

She hesitated, as though she wasn't sure she should voice them. "Only that the...way I feel toward you isn't going to change."

There was a grim sort of satisfaction knowing that. It didn't solve anything, but it soothed his battered ego to hear her admit this wasn't just a sexual thing between them, founded on good old-fashioned lust. He'd considered that aspect himself. He'd been without a woman since Sandy's death, and perhaps his body was starting to play cruel tricks on him. It had been a cause for concern, but one quickly dismissed.

"I want a month," he stated decisively.

"I beg your pardon?" She blinked and scooted to the edge of her seat as though she wasn't sure she'd heard him correctly and was straining to understand.

"I need a month. Right now our feelings for each other are running high." That was putting it mildly. A blacksmith's poker was less hot than they were for each other.

"H-how do you mean?"

"No contact except what's absolutely necessary here at the office. Nothing more. Not even a phone call. I want us to remain as separate as we can and still work in the same command."

Catherine considered the suggestion for a moment, then nodded. "That sounds fair."

"I realize it's going to be difficult for us both."

"But necessary," she added, sounding as reluctant as he felt.

"Unfortunately, it is necessary," Royce agreed. "We can't go on the way we have."

"Something's got to be done."

At least on that they were of one accord.

"What about Kelly?" Catherine asked, her beautiful eyes bright with concern.

"Kelly," Royce repeated in a slow exercise. His daughter was a problem. He'd never seen her take to anyone the way she had Catherine. If he was going to force Kelly not to see Catherine for an entire month, he was likely to have a revolt on his hands. Yet he didn't know how he could maintain his distance from Catherine with Kelly spending time with her. He considered the situation a moment longer, then decided. "As you were quick to remind me not so long ago, it wouldn't be fair to punish her for a problem between us."

Catherine lowered her eyes, and her shoulders sagged as though she were greatly relieved. "Thank you."

"We can set up a time now to talk in exactly one month." He leaned forward and flipped forward the pages of his calendar, finding the date and marking it.

She stood, her eyes somber and determined. "One month," she repeated on her way out the door.

Catherine had known from the moment Royce asked for a month's separation that it wasn't going to be easy. What she hadn't understood was exactly how difficult it would be.

She found herself watching him far more than she ever had before, hungry for contact with him. Each time they were in the same room together, her heart was bathed in a strange blend of emotions. On one hand he was her executive officer, the man she'd been trained to obey without question, without hesitation. On the other hand, he was the man she loved. Mere words were an injustice to describe the strength of what she felt for Royce. She ached for him emotionally and physically. Some nights she'd walk into her apartment so mentally exhausted from this silent battle of longing between them that it was all she could do to feed Sambo.

If this time apart was trying for her, and God knew it was, then it was equally difficult for Royce. They never spoke, not unless it was absolutely necessary. Yet they couldn't be anywhere close to each other without that throbbing awareness breaking out between them. They could be standing in a room filled with other people, yet the intimacy between them was as strong as anything Catherine had ever known. The air was thick and the sensations undeniable.

The first test of their self-imposed restriction came within the first week. Commander Dan Parker stopped Catherine outside the building one chilly afternoon. She'd stayed late working on a complicated case, knowing it was safe to do so since Royce had already left the office. Catherine assumed he'd gone down to the jogging track, as was his habit.

"Hello, Catherine," Dan greeted, strolling purposely toward her.

Catherine envied his carefree smile, and despite everything, found herself responding to it. He must have found encouragement in it, because he paused and asked, "Since you've already rejected my offer to the Birthday Ball, how about soothing my battered ego by agreeing to have dinner with me?"

To be honest, Catherine hadn't given the gala event more than a passing thought since the first time he'd mentioned it. She should give some thought to the ball, but her thoughts were far from festive. "Dinner...when?"

"What's wrong with tonight?"

"I can't," she answered automatically. Dan

seemed to be waiting for an excuse, but she had none to offer. "I'm busy," she answered finally. Busy missing Royce. Busy being miserable. Busy pretending how busy I am.

"It is short notice," Dan admitted. "How about tomorrow night then, after work? We'll unwind over drinks."

Catherine had no reason to refuse. She was convinced Dan had guessed her and Royce's feelings for each other, and although it would be out of the question to discuss the situation, Dan might be able to give her some insight into Royce's personality.

"All right," she agreed, but there wasn't a lot of enthusiasm in her voice.

"Five o'clock at the Yachting Club?"

"Sure, that sounds great."

"Come on, I'll walk you to your car," Dan offered, pressing his hand at her elbow. The comfort Catherine felt at his touch, however impersonal, was enough to bring a rush of surprising tears to her eyes. She managed to blink them away, embarrassed at the unexpected show of emotion.

They were walking toward the asphalt lot, when Royce appeared from out of nowhere. He rounded the corner in a dead run and nearly collided with them. He stopped abruptly, his breath coming in deep gasps.

"Sorry," he said, leaned forward and balanced his hands on his knees. "I didn't think there was anyone left around here."

"No problem," Dan assured him.

Slowly Royce straightened. His eyes avoided looking at Catherine. "What are you doing here so late?"

Dan chuckled and possessively moved his hand up Catherine's back to cup her shoulder. "Talking Catherine into having dinner with me, what else?" Dan joked. "You don't honestly believe I'd stick around this late for Navy business, do you?"

Although everything seemed perfectly normal on the surface, Catherine was well aware of the way Royce's body tensed. The undercurrent between them was so strong she was about to drown in it.

"I see," Royce said, his smile decidedly forced. "I take it our very capable attorney has agreed."

"Not without my having to twist her arm, but once again the Parker charm has won out."

Royce raised his hand in a friendly gesture. "Then don't let me delay you any longer," he said cheerfully. "Have a good time."

"We're going to have a great time," Dan returned, squeezing Catherine's shoulder.

"Good night," Royce said, looking away, but

before his eyes left them, Catherine noted that he dragged his gaze across her lips.

"'Night," Dan murmured. The minute Royce was out of view, he demurely dropped his arm. "I'll meet you tomorrow," he said, grinning, and left.

Catherine stood exactly where she was for several seconds. She didn't know what game Dan Parker was playing, let alone the rules. All she did know was that she had to speak to Royce. Had to explain why she'd agreed to spend time with Dan Parker.

Royce had gone into the building, and not standing around to debate the wisdom of her actions, she followed him inside.

She found him sitting at his desk, his back to her as he stared off into the distance.

"Royce," she said softly, wondering if it would have been better to greet him formally.

He didn't answer her. The silence seemed to stretch for a hundred miles.

"Royce?" she tried again. "Could we talk for just a minute? I know we agreed not to, but I feel…I wanted you to know why I…"

"I already know why," he said in a loud voice, then lowered his voice and swiveled his chair around. "There's no need to explain."

"But…" To her he looked so pale, beaten. Vulnerable.

"We agreed on one month," he reminded her, but the words didn't come easily from his lips.

"Yes, I know." Still she couldn't make herself leave. It felt so good to be in the same room with him, to talk even if it was only for a few moments on a subject that was painful to them both.

Blue eyes sparred with deep, dark ones in a silent, loving battle of wills.

"Catherine, for the love of God, just leave," he begged in a whisper.

"I can't...."

"As your XO I demand that you go."

The silence returned, this time punctuated with pain. Knowing she was defeated, Catherine crisply saluted, turned and abruptly left.

Catherine didn't see Royce for the next three days. Her appointment with Dan, she hesitated to call it a date, was much ado about nothing. He was charming, undemanding and a perfect gentleman the entire time. Not once did he raise the subject of Royce, and for that, Catherine was grateful enough to agree to see him again sometime soon. They left the date open, another fact for which Catherine was thankful.

Time had never passed so slowly. Catherine had come to her decision the first week. She loved Royce, and wanted to be his wife. What they'd need to do to arrange their marriage, if indeed that was what Royce chose, was another matter entirely. She loved him, she loved Kelly, but she loved the Navy, too.

As did Royce.

Being a part of the military was more than their career choice, it was a way of life each had freely embraced. Her commission was just as important to her as Royce's was to him. Both their careers were bright, with room for advancement. Several years down the road, Catherine could easily envision Royce progressing through the ranks. For her part, Catherine hoped to become a judge. Falling in love, marrying and having a family shouldn't mean they had to jeopardize their careers.

It did mean changes would have to be made, however. Complex changes, as complicated as their love for each other.

Catherine's thoughts were interrupted by the phone. Sambo wove his furry, overfed body between her feet as she stood in the kitchen in front of the can opener. While still holding the can of moist cat food, she reached for the phone. Her intention was to continue feeding Sambo, who could be downright insistent, and talk at the same time.

"Hello."

"Catherine?"

She immediately recognized the small, trembling voice as belonging to Kelly.

"What's the matter?" she asked immediately.

"I'm not afraid."

"Of course you're not," Catherine said, abandoning the cat food entirely. "Tell me what's wrong."

"Dad's not here."

"Yes, I know." Royce was away at scheduled meetings for most of the week. "Isn't Cindy or one of the other neighbor girls with you?" Whenever Royce was going to be away, he paid one of the high-school girls in the neighborhood to come and stay with Kelly.

"Cindy's supposed to be."

"But she's not?" Catherine pried gently.

"Her mom's sick and needs her there. Cindy called and wanted me to go over to her house, but I didn't want to do that because I don't want the flu. I hate throwing up."

Catherine grinned, empathizing with that. "I don't blame you, but there really should be someone with you."

"I'm ten years old!" Kelly declared forcefully. "I'm not a baby anymore."

"I know, sweetheart, but there's no telling how long your father's going to be and it's much more fun to have someone stay with you than to be alone."

"Are you alone?"

That was a trick question if Catherine ever heard one. "Sambo's with me."

"A-are you afraid in the dark?" The question was made in the same trembling voice Kelly had used earlier.

"Sometimes," Catherine admitted. "Why?"

"B-because all the lights went out."

Catherine's heart tripped with concern. "You mean to tell me you're all alone in the dark?" Somehow she managed to curtail her anxiety.

"Yes." Once again Kelly's voice was small and weak. "I'm sure the electricity will come back soon, it's just that it's so-o dark."

"Your dad will be there anytime." Catherine hoped some confidence leaked into her voice. The thought of Kelly pretending to be brave brought out a strong motherly instinct in Catherine.

"Dad's probably on his way now," Kelly said, but she didn't sound any too sure of it. "But in case he isn't...do you think you could come over and stay with me until he gets here? I'm not afraid, really I'm not...I'm just a little bit lonely." She paused and sucked in a deep breath. "It wouldn't be too much trouble for you to come, would it?"

Catherine didn't so much as hesitate. "I'll be there in ten minutes." She hung up the receiver and had already reached for her coat when Sambo reminded her he had yet to be fed. Hurrying across the kitchen, Catherine placed the can of food directly on the floor. Sambo was appeased, but he let it be known he didn't appreciate her haphazard methods of serving him his evening meal.

When Catherine arrived, her headlights silhouetted Kelly, standing in the window with the drapes pulled back, waiting. The minute Catherine turned off the engine, the drape swished back into place. Kelly was standing at the front door waiting for her.

"Hello, sweetheart," Catherine greeted.

Kelly's small arms circled her waist and hung on tightly. "I'm glad you're here. I'm not scared or anything."

"Yes, I know," Catherine said, a smile curving the corners of her mouth. The house was pitch-black. "When did the electricity go off?"

"Just a little before I called you." Kelly aimed the flashlight across the living room. "Dad keeps this one handy in the top kitchen drawer, and I found it right away."

"You were a clever girl."

"You really think so?" Kelly sounded proud of herself.

With her hand on Royce's daughter's shoulder, they advanced into the family room and sat down on the sectional together. Kelly chatted easily, as though it had been ages and ages since they'd last talked, which in fact had been several days.

There was a peacefulness that settled over the area, and the dark, which had once seemed so intimidating and uninviting, began to feel like a welcome friend.

Kelly must have sensed it, too. She placed the back of her hand against her mouth and yawned loudly.

"Are you tired?"

"Not really," Kelly answered just before she yawned a second time, but she snuggled closer to Catherine, propping her head in Catherine's lap. Within minutes the measured, even sounds of Kelly's breathing convinced her the girl was sound asleep.

Catherine must have drifted off herself, because the next thing she knew the lights were on. Straightening, she rubbed the sleep from her face just as Royce walked in from the kitchen.

He stopped abruptly and frowned. "What are you doing here?"

Ten

"Kelly was alone," Catherine explained in a husky whisper. "The lights went out and she was afraid." Royce looked shocked, as though he were viewing a ghost. She was certainly the last person he expected to stumble upon in his own home.

Carefully, so as not to waken the slumbering youngster, Catherine gingerly moved from the sectional. She reached for her coat and purse. "Now that you're here, I'll go." She removed the afghan from the back of the sectional and spread it across Kelly, who was dozing peacefully.

"What happened to Cindy?" Royce wanted to know before she left. His mouth had twisted into a tight line of impatience, and Catherine didn't doubt that the teenager was out of a job.

"Her mother came down with a bad case of the flu and she needed her there. She did phone and ask Kelly to walk over to her house."

"It's six blocks. I don't want my daughter traipsing around in the dark." Once more his mouth tightened.

"Kelly didn't go because she hates throwing up."

Royce frowned.

"She didn't want to catch the flu," Catherine explained.

The tight features relaxed, and the two shared a warm smile that seemed to arch between them like two ends of a magical rainbow. It had been so long since they'd shared something so intimate. So long since they'd lowered their guards to allow themselves the simple pleasure. Their eyes met and held for the longest moment. Their breaths seemed to echo each other's. Half a room separated them, and yet it was as though they were standing close enough to touch. A thought Catherine found infinitely appealing. There was security in Royce's arms. Security and love.

It was Royce who dragged his eyes away. His hands were buried deep within his pockets. Catherine would have liked to believe he'd placed them there to keep from reaching for her.

"It was good of you to come by," Royce said evenly.

"It wasn't any problem." The only problem was loving him so much and having to pretend otherwise, even when they were alone together. Such pretense went against the very core of her nature.

Royce followed her into the entryway, stepped ahead, then paused, his hand on the doorknob. His back was to her when he hesitated. "How was your dinner with Dan?"

The question caught her by surprise. Idle curiosity was the last thing she expected from Royce. In addition, she'd nearly forgotten that she'd ever gone out with the commander.

"Forget I asked that," Royce stated gruffly, and jerked open the door.

"Dinner was very good. The company, however, was charming, but decidedly uninteresting."

Royce raked his fingers through his hair and kept his gaze lowered. "Are you going out with him again?"

"No."

Royce's eyes, round and dubious, flew up to meet hers. "Why not?"

Catherine felt as though the weight of the entire world were pressing down upon her shoulders. Royce honestly seemed to need to know why she had no interest in dating another man. Had she been so lacking in communicating her love? Had she failed in letting him know that he was the very reason she lived and breathed?

Didn't he understand that she was prepared to risk everything that was important to her for him?

"You want to know why I'm not dating Dan?" she asked, having trouble hiding how incredible she found the question. "Because, you idiot," she said, battling the urge to sock him, "I'm in love with you."

Royce stood directly in front of her, blocking the door. His eyes, his beautiful blue eyes, drank thirstily from hers, as if it had been years instead of hours since he'd last seen her.

"I shouldn't have asked that." His words were low and dark, laced with a thread of anger, as though he was furious with himself for his lack of control.

"It doesn't matter, really it doesn't," she countered softly, her voice as thin and delicate as the fluttering of her heart.

"Your love matters to me." His eyes lowered to linger on her mouth.

Catherine thought she'd go crazy if he didn't soon kiss her. She wanted him so much that she could taste the desire building within her. It circled her like a binding rope, imprisoning her.

Royce lifted his hand, and his movements were so slow and deliberate. He touched her face, his fingers gently caressing her cheek as if he were blind and was acquainting himself with her. His touch, so light and tender, seemed to reach all the way to her soul. Nothing could have prepared her for the utter beauty of it, the sheer magnitude of these precious, silent moments.

Royce must have felt it, too, the intensity of it. The beauty of it. He was breathing hard when he pulled his hand away, much too hard for such a nondemanding task.

"Thank you for coming," he said, jerking the door open.

"Royce." She wouldn't let him send her away, not again. Not when she needed him so desperately.

"Please...just go." The words were wrenched from him. Sagging with defeat, Catherine did as he requested.

Catherine had dreaded the Birthday Ball all week. She wasn't in any mood to celebrate. Nor was she in the frame of mind to socialize and stand idly by while Royce waltzed around the room with one woman after another. Not when she so longed to be the one in his arms.

She hadn't talked to him since the night she'd gone to be with Kelly. These days were by far the most miserably long ones of her life. It was as if their brief moments together had been ripped out of time. Royce hadn't spoken to her, hadn't looked at her, hadn't acknowledged her.

Catherine had talked to Kelly only once on the phone, hungering all the while for some word from Royce. Something. Anything.

The situation didn't seem to be going any better for him. In the past few days he'd been in one bear of a mood. Half the time it seemed as if he was looking for an excuse to slam his fist through a wall. He wore his bad-boy image as tightly as a glove. It fit him well.

It had taken Catherine only one week of this trial time to make several valid perceptions. She now accepted the fact she was in love with Royce Nyland. But she'd known that before this self-imposed restriction.

She'd also realized that if he asked her to marry him, even if the proposal came on the tail end of a bout of jealousy, or a bout of anything, she'd accept.

What she hadn't anticipated was this heart-wrenching loneliness. The silence that had once fit so comfortably in her life, she now found deafening and painfully disturbing. The pleasure of her own company was sadly lacking. A hundred times, in a hundred different ways she found herself missing Royce even more than she had in the beginning. Since the night with Kelly, she missed the looks they'd often shared, the strong communication between them that made words superfluous. The throaty sound of his laughter. Oh, how she loved hearing him laugh.

She saw him every day, walked past him, spoke to him as if he meant nothing to her, as if they were little more than casual acquaintances. If she found it hard to continue the sham before, it was doubly so now. Painfully so.

Following through with this charade was difficult enough during the day, but to purposely expose herself to it for this Birthday Ball was a challenge she dreaded.

Catherine was forced to admit, however, how beautiful everything was. The orchestra was playing on the opposite end of the room while a mirrored ball hung overhead, casting reflections of warm light about the room. Romance, music, muted light surrounded the couples that circled the polished dance floor. From a distance they resembled graceful swans coasting on a mirrored lake. It was all so beautiful. So splendid.

Catherine stood on the outer edges of the crowd and looked on, admiring the handsome men dressed in either their dress uniforms or tuxedos. The women wore a variety of gowns. Catherine had chosen to wear the formal evening dress uniform with a long straight skirt of navy blue, with matching jacket.

It wasn't until she'd arrived that she understood her choice of outfit for the evening. She needed to remember she was in the Navy. All too often of late, she'd wanted to disregard the pledges she'd made when she accepted her commission. Love seemed far more important than the rules and regulations, which only went to prove how dangerously shaky her thinking was becoming. Royce was right. They needed this time apart, and since he seemed determined to use every one of these thirty days, she had no recourse but to stand by patiently until he'd come to a decision.

Catherine arrived. Royce noticed her the moment she walked in the door. It was as if everything came to a sudden, grinding halt. The music faded, the dancers went still, even the lights seemed to have dimmed. Royce stood, frozen. An air-raid alarm wouldn't have budged him. He simply stood and watched her, soaking in every delicate nuance of her. She was lovely, so breathtakingly lovely that she quite literally held him spellbound. He'd missed her. Dear Lord, how he'd missed her. He felt as though it had been a thousand years since he'd held her in his arms, a thousand years since he'd tasted her lips. Royce was so damned hungry for her that he would have gratefully accepted a few stolen moments alone even if it meant sitting in the front seat of his Porsche on a lonely deserted road.

"Evening, Nyland."

Royce turned to find himself face-to-face with Admiral Duffy. "Good evening, sir," he said, having trouble even then pulling his eyes away from Catherine.

Catherine found herself scanning the dancers, watching, searching. She wasn't fooling herself, she knew who she was looking to find. She didn't see Royce, at least not at first. It wasn't until later, after she'd gotten herself a cup of punch and was wandering around chatting with casual acquaintances that she found him.

He was across the room from her, involved in a conversation with two other men. The first was the admiral, she could tell that much. The second man was turned at an angle so Catherine couldn't identify him, not that it mattered. Royce captured her full attention.

She knew she was cheating on their promise to each other to be watching him the way she was. But the pleasure she found compensated by far for any feelings of guilt.

Royce was different from when she'd first met him, she mused, extraordinarily pleased by the realization. The changes had been subtle over the weeks, but nevertheless they were there. His features remained harsh, though they relaxed more often into a smile than they used to. He would always possess the same rugged appeal, that wasn't likely to ever change. But there was now a serenity about him, she noted, that had been missing when they'd first met, a tranquillity.

Again Catherine experienced a greedy sense of pride, knowing her love was what had made the difference.

"Lieutenant Commander."

The voice behind her was friendly and familiar. "Good evening, Elaine."

Her secretary was dressed in a red velvet gown and stood next to a tall middle-aged lieutenant, who Catherine recognized immediately as Elaine's husband. "This is my husband, Ralph Perkins."

"How do you do?" Catherine said, extending a hand to the man who played such a large role in her secretary's life. "Your wife is as valuable as my right hand."

"Oh, I know," Ralph said in a smooth Southern drawl that caused Catherine to think of antebellum homes with wide sweeping lawns and warm pecan pie fresh from the oven. "I couldn't get along without her, myself."

The three chatted a few minutes longer, before Elaine and her husband headed for the dance floor. For a few moments, Catherine watched them, envious of their freedom to express their love and enjoyment of each other. As she continued to hold on to her punch glass, Catherine's gaze drifted to the floor while she gathered her strength. She was going to need it if she were to make it through this night. When she felt strong enough, she looked over to where she'd last seen Royce.

He was gone. Experiencing a momentary sense of anxiety, she glanced around the room. She couldn't find him anywhere. She searched once again, scanning the crowded ballroom, her gaze moving from one area to another until she happened to catch a glimmer of dark hair and blue eyes when he swirled past her.

Royce was dancing, Catherine realized. Dancing. And it wasn't likely that it was the admiral in his arms.

Catherine had to stop and carefully analyze her feelings. Envy. She would have dearly loved to be the woman in Royce's arms. But she doubted that they would have been able to pull it off. Not tonight, not here with the admirals and captains and all the big mucky-mucks looking on. She was envious, yes, but not jealous.

Royce circled past her a second time, the music crescendoing to a loud climax. Immediately Catherine recognized the white-haired woman in his arms as Admiral Duffy's wife. She felt a little better, knowing the woman was happily married and had been for thirty years. It was little comfort, damn little, but it helped.

Her eyes were on Royce when she felt someone move next to her. "Hello, Catherine."

"Good evening, Dan," she greeted, doing her best to sound friendly. Despite the fact Dan enjoyed playing the role of devil's advocate, Catherine couldn't help liking him. He knew how she felt about Royce and was probably equally knowledgeable of Royce's feelings toward her. But the three of them chose to pretend otherwise. It was amazing when she stopped to think about it.

"Have you saved a dance for me?"

"I…I…"

"More excuses?" he asked with a knowing smile.

"If you don't mind, I'd rather sit this one out."

"My heart is mortally wounded, but I'm becoming accustomed to you knocking my ego around like a tennis ball."

Catherine grinned at the image that sprang readily to her mind. If anyone's heart had been abused, it was her own. And Royce's. Involuntarily, her gaze moved back to him. He really did look…

* * *

…she looked distressed. It was ridiculous to waltz around the dance floor with the admiral's wife in his arms and calculate every step so he could watch Dan Parker make a move on Catherine. Ridiculous or not, that was exactly what Royce was doing.

At one time, he'd actually encouraged Dan to ask Catherine out. It had been a futile attempt to stop what was happening between him and Catherine. He couldn't believe he'd done anything so stupid. It wouldn't have worked. There'd never been the slightest possibility of that, but at the time he'd been desperate. He could still remember how angry Catherine had been at him, how she'd walked into his office, her eyes sparking with outrage and fury.

A good deal of water had passed under the bridge since then. The waters of discernment, the waters of perception. What he felt for Catherine was real. Strong. Heady. He hadn't meant to fall in love. He'd avoided love for years. Struggled with it, contested the fact it was possible for a man and woman to truly love each other. His first taste of it had left a bitter aftertaste, and he wasn't eager to experience it again.

"You needn't have turned Dan down, you know."

Breathless emotion clenched Catherine's

heart when she realized it was Royce who was speaking to her. She whirled around to discover him standing only a few feet away.

"It wouldn't have mattered," he assured her.

Her heart beat mercilessly against her ribs. She blinked as though she wasn't sure she should trust herself not to have conjured him up. Her emotions were exhausted. Her nerves shot. This charade was killing her in inches.

"Shall we?" Royce held out his arms to her.

Catherine didn't question the right or wrong of them holding each other on the dance floor. Nor did she object when he slipped his arms around her waist. It was as though they'd been partnering each other for years. Their bodies were in perfect sync, they moved in flawless harmony, swaying naturally, rhythmically to the music.

Catherine's eyes held his, so greedy for the opportunity to study him that she didn't care what he could read in her eyes or who saw them. Nothing mattered but Royce. Her life had been a confused jumble from the time she'd first met Royce Nyland. Why should anything be different now?

"Why do you have to be the most beautiful woman here tonight?" Royce whispered the question close to her ear.

"It's in the genes, what can I tell you?" Catherine teased, and was rewarded by the feel of his mouth smiling against her hair. She knew he was holding her closer than he should, but she couldn't bring herself to ease away.

"I'd give everything I possess to be able to kiss you right now."

Catherine's response was half moan, half sigh. Unfortunately, she was feeling much the same thing herself. She dared to look into his eyes and was rewarded with the promise of sensual delights. For sanity's sake she quickly looked away, but it didn't prevent a hot flush to her cheeks.

"I don't think it's a good idea for you to say things like that…at least not here."

"Oh, and why's that?"

"Royce," she groaned, "you know why. Oh, stop, please stop…someone might notice." His hands were on her waist, and he was dragging her even closer, to a more solid intimacy. Her body was aligned with his in such a way, she could feel every subtle, and not so subtle, part of him.

"Let them look," Royce challenged, his words a low growl in her ear.

"But…"

His lips brushed her cheek. "Do you think I care?"

"Yes," she cried. "We both care."

"Not anymore." Once again his lips bounced lightly against her forehead.

"What…do you mean?"

"I mean there're reasons for us to do this sort of thing without worry, without fearing the consequences."

Catherine's heart clashed like two giant cymbals beating together. Holding her breath, she eased her head back so she could examine his face. His eyes readily met hers, and Catherine gasped softly at what she saw. Love. A love so strong and so determined that it would survive whatever they had yet to face. Royce loved her, with a love that defied logic, defied description. A love that was destined to be the moving force behind what remained of their lives. Neither one of them would ever be the same. Neither one of them would want to be the same.

"I love you so damn much."

Catherine closed her eyes to battle back a flood of feelings so strong they threatened to overwhelm her.

"We're getting married," he announced next.

The very eyes that had drifted shut only a moment earlier, shot open. "When? How?"

Royce laughed, that same throaty, hoarse laugh that had haunted her sleep for nearly two weeks. "I haven't got that part figured out yet, but I'm working on it. It seems, my dear, sensible wife-to-be that I'm about to be transferred."

"When? Where?"

"That's something else that has yet to be decided, but it's in the works."

He was so close, too close, but she needed that, needed the reality of him holding her in his arms even if they were supposed to be dancing. The fact their feet were barely moving didn't seem to concern either of them.

"When did you find out?"

"Tonight," he told her. "Shortly after you arrived. I was watching you, wanting you so much my heart was about to burst wide open when Admiral Duffy decided now was as good a time to tell me my request had been granted. He'd apparently been in contact with the detailers in Washington, D.C."

"You asked for a transfer...you never said—"

"I couldn't go on the way we were."

"Oh, Royce." She'd been watching him this evening, too. She longed to tell him how she'd looked for him the moment she arrived, hungry for the sight of him. But her throat was too thick. She'd tell him later when she could speak without the threat of tears.

"I want you, Catherine, by my side for the next fifty years. I want to make love to you so often they'll need another category in *The*

Guinness Book of Records. When I wake up in the mornings, I want you sleeping at my side."

"Oh, Royce."

"Right now I want to kiss you so damn much that I'd be willing to risk shocking every man and woman in this room." His voice had grown reedy with impatience. "Let's get out of here before I do forget where we are and do exactly as my instincts demand."

"Oh, Royce."

"Frankly," he teased, his mouth tantalizingly close to her ear, "I don't remember you having such a limited vocabulary." The music stopped, but he didn't release her. If anything his hold grew more possessive.

"Royce," she hissed, "be good." She feared anyone even remotely glancing at them would immediately know what they felt for each other.

"I want to be bad," he whispered seductively. "Do you want to be bad with me?"

"Oh, yes…"

"Good, then we agree. Now let's leave before someone arrests me for thinking what I'm thinking."

Slowly, with enough reluctance to make her heart long to sing, Royce lowered his arms and released her. "Get your coat and meet me in the parking lot." A lazy grin slashed his mouth. "By now I'm sure you know which car is mine."

"Royce, I...do you honestly think..." Catherine pulled herself up short. "Just exactly how bad do you want to be?"

He chuckled. "I love it when you blush. I don't think I've ever found a woman more appealing than you are right this moment."

"I think you're crazy."

"We both are."

He left her then, hurrying across the room to make his excuses and gather his own coat. Catherine didn't linger. Within a few moments she was outside, searching through a sea of parked cars for Royce's. Before she could spot his black Porsche, he pulled to a fast stop directly in front of her.

The passenger door opened, and Catherine slipped inside. She had barely had time to sit down when Royce reached for her chin, directing her mouth to his for a surprisingly brief, but thorough kiss.

"Royce," she cried, alarmed. "What are you doing?"

"Kissing you." He took advantage of her open mouth by giving her a fleeting taste of his tongue. Despite the fact there could be several important people watching them who wouldn't take kindly to this public display of affection between two officers, one subordinate to the other, Catherine found herself drifting toward him.

"Hold on," he said, shifting gears so hard and fast they ground angrily. The car shot forward. Royce didn't take her far. Just to the other end of the parking lot where it was dark and private. "There's no need to be so impatient," he said, reaching for her even as he spoke. "You're going to have the opportunity to make love to me every night for the rest of our lives."

Eleven

"Have you gone out of your mind?" Catherine demanded with a free-flowing happiness that refused to be contained.

Royce eased to a stop at the red light, leaned over and kissed her soundly. Once more he used his tongue to tantalize and tease. His eyes were closed when he pulled away. "I am crazy," he murmured, unwilling to deny it, "crazy in love with you."

Catherine felt as though she were in a haze. "I can't believe this is happening."

"Believe it."

The light changed, but Catherine was convinced that, had it stayed red much longer, Royce would have reached for her a second time.

"Just where are you taking me?" The joy seemed to bubble out of her like fizz from an expensive bottle of champagne. If Royce had claimed he was headed for the moon, she would have held on for the ride.

"My house," he told her without hesitating.

"Your house," she repeated slowly.

"Kelly's going to want to be in on this. If we wait until morning to tell her, she'll be furious." Royce's gaze momentarily drifted away from the road, and his rugged features relaxed into a coaxing smile. "I'm convinced Kelly knew there was going to be something between us even before we did."

Catherine sighed and rested her head against the hard cushion of Royce's shoulder. It felt so incredibly good to be with him, so incredibly wonderful. There was nothing in this world to describe it.

A couple of minutes later, Royce eased his Porsche to a stop in his driveway. He turned off the engine and in one smooth movement reached for her. He kissed her hard and fast, and Catherine kissed him back with every ounce of her being.

Royce moaned as he deepened the contact. His tongue dipped to hungrily drink from her love. His hands were in her hair, and when he drew himself away, it was as though he were forcing himself to walk away from the gates of paradise.

"Let's go inside," he suggested, as though they'd best do it soon or else pay the piper.

Catherine nodded. At the moment, formulating words was beyond her passion-drugged brain.

The babysitter, a neighborhood teenager, was slouched across the sectional in the family room, watching television and drinking Pepsi. She looked mildly surprised to see Royce home so early. Her gaze left Royce and rested with candid curiosity on Catherine.

"Kelly's asleep," the teenager explained, her gaze drifting away from Catherine long enough to speak to Royce.

"Fine, thanks for coming, Cindy," Royce said, pulling out the money to pay her. He walked her to the door, opening it for her. "Goodbye, now."

"Bye." Cindy peeked around the door at Catherine one last time. She raised her hand. "Bye," she said, directing the comment to her.

"Bye," Catherine said, raising her fingertips.

Royce eased the door closed and locked it after the teenager. When he turned back, his smile was gone. He murmured something Catherine couldn't understand. "I apologize for not introducing you, but there's a very good reason I don't want Cindy to know who you are." He rammed all ten fingers through his hair in an exercise of ill-gained patience. "Although heaven knows she's probably already guessed."

"Don't worry about it." Catherine stepped forward and pressed the tips of her fingers over his mouth. It didn't take much for her to figure out that Cindy was the daughter of someone who could make trouble for them. "I'm not going to let anything or anyone ruin this night."

Gripping her by the shoulders, Royce braced his forehead against hers. "Have I told you how much I love you?"

"Yes, but I'd be willing to listen to it again if you're inclined to tell me."

"I'm inclined," he murmured, his mouth brushing hers. "Get ready because it's going to take me a lifetime to say it properly."

They kissed again. The moment was gentle and sweet, so sweet that Catherine had trouble believing everything that was happening between them was real.

"I better get Kelly," Royce said, unwillingly easing himself from her. "While I still have the strength to pull away from you."

Catherine didn't know who found it more difficult, Royce or her.

"Wait here," Royce said, positioning her at the bottom of the carpeted stairs. "I'll be back in just a moment." He kissed her once more and raced up the stairs, taking them two and three at a time. Catherine could hear Royce talking to Kelly, but as far as she could tell the conversation was strictly one-sided.

Royce appeared at the top of the stairs a few moments later, a sleeping Kelly draped over his shoulder. The youngster had on her robe, one patterned with the faces of her favorite rock group, and her feet were dangling with hastily donned fuzzy slippers.

"Kelly?" Catherine coaxed softly. "Your father and I have something important to tell you."

Yawning, the sleepy-eyed girl slowly lifted her head from her father's shoulder. "Catherine?"

"I told you she was here," Royce reminded his daughter.

Rubbing her eyes with small fists, Kelly straightened. "But you said Catherine couldn't come over anymore. I'm not supposed to phone her or even say her name unless you tell me it's all right first."

Royce looked downright chagrined. He cast an apologetic glance to Catherine, cleared his throat and explained, "Your name came up far too often."

"No, it didn't," Kelly denied, placing her head back down on Royce's shoulder as he carried her down the stairs.

"That's all going to change," Catherine told the youngster. "Real soon."

"I asked Catherine if she'd marry me, and she's agreed," Royce said. A brilliant smile sat contentedly at the edges of his mouth.

Kelly's head came off Royce's shoulder so fast it was downright comical. "You're going to marry Catherine?" she cried, then squeezed her dad around the neck. Royce's shining eyes met Catherine's, and he stuck out his tongue as though he were in danger of being strangled.

"Oh, Catherine, I'm so happy." Kelly broke away from her father, twisted around and reached for Catherine, squeezing her equally hard. "I can't believe it! This is the happiest day of my whole, entire life. I'm not dreaming, am I?"

"No, sweetheart," Royce said, sharing an intimate look with Catherine, "this is very real." He set a squirming Kelly down on the carpet.

"This is great. This is *really* great." Kelly slapped her hands hard against the sides of her legs. "What I want to know is what took you guys so long?"

"Ah…" Catherine hesitated.

"I realize there were a few minor problems, but as far as I could see you both stretched everything way out of proportion. Heaven knows how long it would have taken you to come to your senses if it hadn't been for me."

"That's true," Royce agreed, looking to Catherine and poignantly rolling his eyes. He moved to her side and slipped his arm around her shoulder with a casual easiness that suggested he'd been doing so for a good long while. "The thing is, sweetheart," Royce said, his eyes dark and serious, "we're going to have to keep this a secret. Understand?" The entire wedding would need to be handled discreetly.

Kelly nodded, then pretended to zip her lip closed.

"When?" Kelly demanded.

Royce's gaze caught Catherine's. "Soon, I hope."

"Great. Now, listen, we don't have a whole lot of time to waste with this." The ten-year-old stalked into the living room, sat down and crossed her legs. "Well, come here," she said, gesturing for them to follow her.

Catherine and Royce stared blankly at each other.

"Come here," Kelly repeated when they hesitated. "We don't have all night, you know."

"Exactly what is it you want to talk to us about?" Royce demanded.

"What else is there to discuss?" Kelly cried. "My baby sister!"

"Ah…" Catherine's gaze darted to Royce, who did a good job of looking as stumped as she. Children. Kelly wanted to discuss enlarging their family when they hadn't decided on a wedding date. Good heavens, Catherine had yet to figure out how they were going to pull this whole shenanigan off without anyone from the base finding out, and Kelly wanted to discuss a baby sister.

Royce's arm circled Catherine's waist as they moved into the formal living room. "What's the matter, darling, has the cat got your tongue?"

"A baby sister," Catherine repeated slowly, thoughtfully. She didn't want to burst Kelly's bubble, but at the same time the ten-year-old needed to be aware that there were several things to consider before they discussed a pregnancy.

Catherine sat down on the bronze velvet sofa. Royce sat slightly behind her, his arms circling her waist. "I was hoping we could talk about other matters," Catherine suggested, thinking of a tactful way of changing the subject.

"We could." Kelly was willing to concede that much. "I can be the flower girl, can't I?"

"Anything you want." Catherine hadn't gotten around to thinking that far ahead, but she certainly didn't have any objections if that was what Kelly wanted.

"I was thinking pink."

"Pink?" Royce repeated as though he'd never heard the word before. "Pink what?"

"For the wedding colors, of course." Kelly tossed him a look that suggested his presence wasn't at all necessary, at least not right then. "You look real pretty in pink, Catherine, and it's a nice omen."

"Omen?" This time it was Catherine who couldn't find her way around Royce's fast-talking daughter.

"For my baby sister."

"Of course, how silly of me." Catherine was beginning to feel that Kelly wasn't so much interested in gaining a mother as she was looking for a vehicle to deliver her long-awaited sibling.

"What if we have a son first?" Catherine wanted to know. She should find out these things just in case Kelly intended to boot her out of the family for having delivered something other than the specified request.

Kelly wrinkled her nose as if she found the mere suggestion distasteful. "I suppose a boy would be all right. I've heard lots of talk from the girls at school about how dads really like having sons. Personally, I'd much prefer a sister, but I guess this is just one of those things that we'll leave up to God."

"I have no idea where she comes up with this stuff," Royce whispered for Catherine's benefit.

"Does this mean we're moving?" Kelly wanted to know next, her look pensive.

Royce went tense behind Catherine. She realized this was the part Royce dreaded most. Bangor was the only Navy base Kelly had ever known, although Royce had been stationed in other Puget Sound bases. Uprooting his daughter had been Royce's primary concern about the two of them marrying. "More than likely we'll be moving."

After having a good deal to say about everything else, Kelly simply nodded.

"Does that bother you?" Catherine asked.

"Not really. Lots of other kids in my school have lived all over the world. Everyone says that if you join the Navy you get shipped everywhere. I think it's our turn. Actually, when you think about it, it's time we left Bangor."

"I don't know where we're going yet."

"But where do you think?" Kelly pressed.

"I'm hoping to be assigned to the Navy station in Bremerton, but we can't count on that."

"Really!" Kelly jumped off the couch and clapped her hands. "That'd be great. We could move to Catherine's apartment and Sambo could sleep with me and it'd hardly be moving at all."

"But we can't count on that. Admiral Duffy's promised to see what he can do."

"Where else?"

"There's always a chance I'll go to Pensacola, Florida."

Once again Kelly was on her feet clapping wildly. "All right, Disney World here I come."

"Sweetheart," Royce said, looking more than a little surprised by his daughter's reaction to the possibility of moving across the country. "Just remember, I haven't a clue where we're headed. So we should be prepared for anything."

"Does it matter where we move?" Kelly asked with a sanguine smile. "Catherine will be with us."

"Maybe," Royce corrected.

Kelly's bright blue eyes narrowed suspiciously. She set her fists against her hip bones and glared across the room. "Exactly what do you mean by that?"

"First we have to find out where your father's going to be stationed," Catherine explained, loving the expressive way Kelly had of letting her feelings be known. "Then I need to request a transfer there myself, or at least to a base close to where your dad's stationed. We still won't be able to be in the same command, but—"

"What happens if the Navy decides to send Dad one place and you another?"

It was a distinct possibility, and one Catherine prayed they'd never have to consider.

"We'll cross that bridge when we come to it," Royce assured the three of them.

Kelly's nod was profound. "Good thinking." She crossed her arms and leaned back against the sofa. "Now that we've got that out of the way, there are a couple of other things we need to discuss."

"Is that a fact?" Royce said, but the look he shared with Catherine suggested that he was as much at a loss as she.

Kelly cleared her throat, and her face grew dark and serious. "No hanky-panky."

"I beg your pardon." Royce was indignant.

"You heard me." Kelly's index finger shot out in a way that would have made teachers across America proud. "Not until you're married at least. I'm not a little kid anymore," Kelly informed them with a righteous tilt to her chin. "I know what kind of stuff goes on between men and women. I watch MTV."

"I don't believe this is any of your concern, young lady." Royce was frowning, but Catherine wasn't entirely sure what was bothering him; the fact Kelly watched racy music videos, or that she was insisting on curtailing their romantic involvement.

"You wouldn't want to taint my young mind, would you?"

"If I'm going to taint anything, it'll be your backside," Royce announced loudly.

The threat was real enough for Kelly to sit on her hands to protect her posterior.

"This is the same kid who was afraid in a power outage," Catherine whispered to Royce.

"That was a trick."

"She turned off all the lights herself?"

"No," Royce said, and shook his head for emphasis. "She called you over knowing I'd be back any minute, thereby forcing the two of us to deal with each other."

"You always told me it's impolite to whisper," Kelly said indignantly from across the room. She stood, yawned once and headed for the stairs. "I'll be back in just a moment."

"You'll be back?" Royce repeated.

"Of course. I'll need to go with you when you take Catherine home. You don't honestly expect me to stay here alone, do you?"

"Ah…"

"What's the matter, love?" Catherine murmured, flexing her long nails against Royce's arms, which were wrapped securely around her waist. "Has the cat got your tongue?"

"I'll only be a minute," Kelly said, rushing up the stairs.

"Which means..." Royce said, drawing Catherine back on to the thick sofa cushions. He felt solid and strong, and just the feel of him was enough to ease the terrible loneliness that had haunted her for nights on end.

Catherine raised her arms to link them around his neck. His eyes were on her. "So much for us being bad." He lowered his mouth and feasted.

"Ho hum." Kelly coughed loudly, disrupting them a few minutes later. "Not a good idea," she announced. "There's plenty of time for that sort of thing later. Right now we've got a wedding to think about."

"A flower girl," Royce murmured, slowly untangling his arms from around Catherine. "I have a feeling that by the time this wedding takes place, Kelly may be in a boarding school in Switzerland."

The following week was impossible. That was the only way Catherine could think to define it. Knowing Royce was being transferred, but not knowing where made any planning impossible. They couldn't arrange for a wedding until several factors were figured into the equation. First and foremost they needed to know when Royce would be dispatched. The news of his new duty assignment could come at any moment, and Royce could be ordered to ship out with as little as twenty-four-hours notice and as much as six months.

The restrictions upon them were just as stringent as before. As Kelly had so eloquently put it, *no hanky-panky*. Catherine would have paid anything just for the opportunity to "be bad" with Royce, but that, too, was prohibited. They'd come too far to risk everything now.

Catherine was sitting at her desk when Royce strolled into the office. "Lieutenant Commander, could I see you in my office, right away?"

"Yes, sir."

Elaine Perkins scooted back to her chair as Catherine left her office, her secretary's gaze following Royce. "Ol' stoneface seems to be in a pleasant enough mood lately, don't you think?"

"I wouldn't know," Catherine said before she let something slip that she'd soon regret. She'd long suspected that her observant secretary was aware of her feelings for Royce, but it was a subject neither dared broach.

"How can you not have noticed?" Elaine demanded. "I actually saw Commander Nyland smiling the other day. Smiling. Not that I could see there was anything to smile about, but that's not my concern. Up until recently I assumed it would take an act of Congress to get that man to so much as grin. Lately that's all changed."

Catherine didn't comment. "Do you want me

to ask him what he found so amusing? I'll tell him you're curious to find out."

"Funny, Catherine, very funny."

Amused herself, Catherine walked into Royce's office and closed the door. "You wanted to see me?"

"How do you feel about living in Virginia?" he asked without warning. "I've been assigned to Submarine Force, Atlantic Fleet at Norfolk."

"Virginia," she repeated slowly. Her heart was pounding hard. "I'd love Antarctica if I could be there with you."

Royce grinned, and their eyes held each other. "I feel the same way."

"How much time do I have?" She arched her brows expectantly, waiting for him to respond.

"Two weeks."

"Two weeks." Catherine's heart sank as she lowered herself into a chair and closed her eyes. Her mind started buzzing. It wasn't possible. It simply wasn't possible.

But it had to be! She'd do whatever she must to arrange it so they could be married before he was deployed.

"Catherine?"

She was on her feet again and not quite sure how she got there. She blinked once, then smiled over to Royce, confident her smile covered her entire face. "Two weeks," she repeated, and nodded once, willing to accept the challenge. "I've got a whole lot of planning to do."

Royce looked concerned. "I don't want to postpone the wedding." It went without saying that the ceremony would have to be discreet. For the two of them to marry so quickly after Royce was detached from the command would be a problem. They'd discussed it at length and had agreed to fly to San Francisco for the ceremony.

Catherine cast him a look that assured him otherwise. "I don't want to wait, either." They were both well aware that it would be better for them to let several months pass. But neither found that acceptable. "I'll contact my mother right away. She'll help with the arrangements. Personally, I doubt that I'd be able to pull this off without her."

"You can contact the whole state of California if that's what you want. Just as long as you're at the church on time."

"I'll be there, don't you worry."

"Mom, it's Catherine."

"Sweetheart." Her mother's voice was elevated with pleasure. "It's so good to hear from you."

"How's work…I mean, you're not into anything heavy, are you?"

"No more than usual."

"Good." Catherine hesitated. She really would be asking a good deal of her mother, who was a newlywed herself, but there was no help for it.

"Good? Why's that?" Once again her mother's voice was raised with curiosity.

"Because I need you to do something for me…"

"Of course, whatever you need."

"I need your expertise—" She wasn't allowed to finish.

"Catherine, you're a fine lawyer, I'm sure you don't need my opinion, and furthermore I don't think the Navy would take kindly to my interfering in something that has to do with the military."

"Not in the courts, Mom." Catherine couldn't keep from grinning. The happiness was oozing out of her. "Royce asked me to marry him."

"I thought he'd already done that."

"He wasn't serious then, only jealous."

"I take it he's serious this time?"

"Very serious. He arranged for a transfer before he proposed. He's been assigned to the submarine base in Virginia. I've put in for a transfer there myself."

"And?" The question came after a noticeable pause.

"And I haven't heard yet. But we want to be married as soon as possible. We can't let anyone know, at least not right away. The whole thing has to be handled delicately."

"Of course. But once you're married, the Navy wouldn't separate a husband and wife, will it?"

"You're joking, Mom?" Catherine asked with a light laugh. "I thought you knew the military better than that. The Navy does what's most convenient for the Navy. Royce and I have no right falling in love in the first place."

"But he'll be in Virginia, and you might well end up stationed in Washington."

"We don't know that yet. Royce is pulling every string he can to make sure that doesn't happen. Even if worse comes to worse and I do have to stay here, it won't be forever. Eventually we'll be together."

"I don't like the sound of this, Catherine," her mother said in low, concerned tones.

"Trust me, it's essential for right now."

"Not necessarily. Sweetheart, don't you think you should consider resigning from the Navy?"

It was an argument Catherine had been having with herself for several days. She'd talked it over with Royce, and they'd batted the idea back and forth several times, but she'd been adamant and he hadn't pressured her. "I'm not leaving the Navy," she argued forcibly with her mother. "I'm not giving up my career just because I happened to fall in love."

"You'll always be an attorney, and frankly, I've never understood why you don't simply join a law firm, you'd do much better financially."

"That's an old argument and not one I'm going to get involved with now. I've come too far to resign now. Besides, of all the people in the world, I would have thought you'd understand my feelings about the Navy. Resigning isn't even up for consideration. Royce knows that and accepts it."

"But, Catherine, sweetheart, be reasonable, what man wants to be separated from his wife by thousands of miles?"

"You're making it sound like a foregone conclusion that I won't be transferred with him. In every likelihood I will, so quit worrying about it," Catherine stated heatedly. She immediately felt contrite. Her mother wasn't telling her something she hadn't already debated long and hard. The Navy was important to both her and Royce. Catherine noted, however, that no one suggested he resign his commission and become a civilian because he wanted to marry her.

"What about children?"

"Mom, I don't think we're gong to accomplish anything productive going over this now. I've got less than two weeks to make all the necessary arrangements. Royce is detaching from his command here, which helps. Can you send us whatever it is we need to file for a wedding license in California?"

"Of course."

"Good." But her mother was right. What about children? Catherine didn't know if she was being greedy to want it all. A career, a family and the Navy. That was a question she had yet to face.

The next few days passed in a whirlwind of frantic activity. Catherine barely saw Royce, barely talked to him. Late in the week he and Kelly flew to Virginia to make the necessary arrangements for housing.

Friday after work, Catherine returned to her apartment in a haze of concern. Over the next two days she spent hours on the phone with her mother, arranging for the florists, photographers and trying on every wedding dress within two counties.

Royce called her late Sunday evening. "Hello, beautiful," he greeted in a soft, sexy voice that curled her toes.

She was exhausted physically and mentally. "Hello yourself," she answered, fighting back a powerful need to have his arms around her.

Instead she forced herself to ask all the right questions. "Did you and Kelly find a house?"

"Within the first day. It's perfect. Three bedrooms, nice family room, a large kitchen and all for a reasonable rent." Royce hadn't been able to obtain housing on the base, which made the move just a little more difficult. Kelly had considered it important to accompany him on this trip so she could scout out the schools and choose the right kind of neighborhood, which meant one with lots of girls her age.

"What did Kelly think of Virginia?"

"It was radical this and radical that. At least that's what I seem to remember her saying. Right now everything's new and fun. I don't think she's going to have any problems making the adjustment."

Catherine snuggled up on the sofa, the phone cord stretched as far as it would go from the kitchen wall. Her gaze rested on the photograph of her father, lingering there for several moments. "Kelly's going to be making a whole lot of adjustments in the next few weeks." It worried Catherine that Royce's daughter was suffering the brunt of the sacrifices they each were forced into making for this marriage.

"Kelly's resilient. Trust me, she would have willingly moved to the jungles of darkest Africa if it meant you were going to be part of our family."

"I love you." Catherine felt the need to say it. It suddenly seemed important for her to voice her feelings.

"I love you, too." After the hectic craziness that had surrounded them for what seemed like months on end, it was good to sit in the solitude of her home and cherish the words she'd longed to hear for so many weeks.

"I didn't want to love you, at least not at first," Royce admitted roughly. "God knows I tried to stay away from you."

"I tried, too."

"I'd give anything to have you in my arms right now."

"That's all going to change soon, and I'll be in your arms for the rest of our lives." She said it as a reminder to herself, wiping the moisture from her cheek. She should be the happiest woman in the world. Within a matter of days she and Royce would be man and wife. Yet the envelope sitting on the corner of her desk was a constant reminder of how quickly that happiness could be tarnished.

Royce paused, and although he must be exhausted, Catherine realized he'd picked up on the fact she was miserably unhappy. She tried so hard to hide it behind busy questions and a cheerful facade.

"Are you going to tell me?" he demanded softly.

"There's no need to spoil everything now. You'll find out soon enough.... You're back safe and sound, and that's what matters. Mission accomplished. Kelly's happy. What more could you possibly want?"

"You."

"Oh, my darling, you have me. You've held on to my heart for weeks on end, don't you know that?"

"I already know, Catherine," he told her softly. "You don't need to hide it from me."

She sucked in her breath. "When did you find out?"

"Friday before I left."

Her request for transfer had been denied. The worst scenario. Her worst nightmare. She was going to be stationed in Bangor while Royce and Kelly were on the other side of the country.

"Oh, Royce," she asked softly, "what are we going to do?"

"Exactly what we're planning. I'm marrying you, Catherine, come hell or high water."

Twelve

The wedding ceremony took place Friday evening in a small San Francisco chapel with the pastor from Marilyn Fredrickson-Morgan's church. The altar was decorated with brilliant red poinsettias, and although Royce wasn't much into flowers, he was impressed with the traditional Christmas flower that crowded every square inch of floor space around the altar. Catherine and her mother had done a beautiful job. Even Kelly who'd first suggested a pink color scheme approved of the festive red bows and other complements.

As for the ceremony itself, Royce remembered little of what progressed. The moment he'd stepped over to join the reverend and viewed Catherine slowly marching down the aisle toward him, he'd been so lost in her loveliness that everything else around him had faded.

Even the small reception afterward with

both families and a few close friends remained hazy in his mind. Catherine fed him a piece of heart-shaped cake bordered with red roses and sipped champagne. They even danced a couple of times.

There had been gifts, too. Royce couldn't get over how many when there were less than fifty people at the entire wedding.

Kelly had been in her element. Royce's parents had flown in from Arizona, along with a couple of his aunts and uncles. Even his younger brother and his family had managed to make it up from the southern part of the state. Kelly had basked in all the attention. She'd taken to Marilyn and Norman almost as quickly as she'd taken to Catherine herself.

His daughter delighted in announcing to any and everyone who would listen that he and Catherine owed everything to her. She'd also sounded like something of a parole officer when she admitted to Catherine's mother that she'd personally seen to it that no hanky-panky had been allowed before the wedding ceremony.

At the moment Catherine was changing clothes, something she'd done once or twice already since the wedding. He couldn't understand why she insisted on dressing when he fully intended on undressing her the minute they arrived at the hotel room he'd booked.

Royce would much rather have chosen someplace romantic for their honeymoon. Unfortunately they weren't going to have a whole lot of time together before he assumed his duties in Virginia. With a limited time schedule, Royce quickly decided he'd rather spend it in bed with Catherine than on the road seeking out the perfect romantic hideaway.

A private room on one of the beaches might have worked out nicely, but the San Francisco hotel offered one advantage the others didn't. Room service.

Royce had two short days with Catherine, and he sure as hell didn't plan on spending any of it sightseeing.

It seemed to take the taxi forever to reach the hotel. They chatted about the wedding, teased and even managed to kiss a couple of times. It wasn't until they'd registered and were on their way up to the honeymoon suite that it hit Royce.

He was nervous.

Royce Nyland jittery! It was almost enough to make him laugh. Marriage wasn't a new experience to him. He'd been through it all before. If anything was different it was the fact he and Catherine had yet to make love.

Sandy had been sleeping with him for months before they'd seriously discussed getting married. Royce wished to hell he'd made love to

Catherine before now. It might have eased the knot twisting his gut.

No it wouldn't, he amended promptly. When it came right down to it, he was glad they'd waited. It hadn't been easy, even with Kelly wagging her finger under their noses at every opportunity.

He didn't need his daughter reminding him to be good, or anyone else for that matter. The Navy had seen to it all on its own. He'd followed the law book, with only a few minor infractions. He'd made the best of a sticky situation. But, by heaven, Catherine was his wife now, and he was ready to attempt a new world's record for lovemaking!

A warm sensation softened his heart. He was doing everything right this time. Right by Catherine. Right by himself. Right by the Navy. There was a gratifying sort of comfort knowing that.

"Are you hungry?" he asked.

"A little." Royce swore she sounded as on edge as he did, which pleased him. At least he wasn't the only one experiencing qualms.

"Do you want to order something from room service?" He found a menu by the phone and scanned the list of entrées. Nothing sounded particularly appetizing, but if Catherine was interested, he'd order something for her.

"I'd be willing to eat something," she said lightly, but Royce wasn't fooled. Dinner was a delay tactic for them both.

They ordered a fancy meal, but Royce noted that neither of them seemed to have much of an appetite once the food arrived. So his gutsy Catherine was nervous, too. Royce found that endearing, and he was charmed by her all the more.

What they really needed to get things rolling, Royce decided when he set the food tray outside their door, was the front seat of a car. The thought produced a wide grin, one he suspected would have made a Cheshire cat proud.

"You're smiling," Catherine said when he returned. "What's so amusing?"

"Us. Come here, woman, I'm tired of pussyfooting around this. I want to make love to you, and I'm not waiting any longer." He held his arms open to her, and she walked toward him, slipping tidily into his embrace. They fit together perfectly. Royce believed they had been created for each other. For a cure for all the lonely, barren years he'd spent alone. Years she'd spent alone.

He kissed her once gently and felt her breath, hot and fiery, against his throat. One kiss and Royce was suddenly as weak as a newborn kitten. It didn't help matters any to have her snuggle against him, her skin silky and warm.

Royce's hands were trembling as he reached for the zipper at the back of her dress. Catherine straightened and raised her arms so he could lift the silky garment over her head. It slipped right off, and she rewarded him for his efforts by trailing her lips over the corded muscles of his neck and shoulders, her tongue slipping over the hollow of his throat.

Royce closed his eyes to the deluge of feelings. His heart started to pound, but that wasn't his only reaction. His whole body had started throbbing. He couldn't remove his clothes fast enough. Once his shirt was free of his waistband, Catherine took over for him, slowly, too slowly to suit him, unfastening the buttons one by one. She sighed softly and fanned her hands across his chest, her nails innocently tugging against the hairs of his chest like a kitten yearning for attention.

"Oh, Royce… Kiss me, please kiss me."

He caught his breath and then did as she asked, spreading hot kisses across her delicate shoulders, then up the side of her exquisite neck until their mouths met in a burst of spontaneous combustion that was so fierce it threatened to consume them both.

Her tongue shyly met his, and he groaned,

the sound rough and masculine to his own ears.
Catherine moaned, too, and it was the most sensual, erotic whimper Royce had ever heard. He
had to touch her, had to feel for himself her excitement, had to taste it and know she wanted
him as desperately as he hungered for her.

His hands massaged her back, and he was
gratified to realize she'd removed her bra. She
leaned into him, absorbing what little strength
he possessed, and looped her arms around his
neck. Royce's hands cupped her breasts. They
were soft and full, so marvelously lush and
round. The nipples instantly pearled, and the
feel of them puckering, hardening, then scrap-
ing against his palms as she moved against him
sent a wave of molten sensation over him.

Royce raised his head and judged the distance
to the bed. Lifting her into his arms, Royce
stalked across the carpet like a warrior haul-
ing his conquest into the middle of camp.

He pressed Catherine onto the mattress and
then joined her, being sure he didn't suffocate
her with his weight.

He kissed her again and again, so many times
he lost count, so many times that she melted
against him, her eyes pleading with him for the
completion they both sought.

Royce couldn't wait another moment, another
second. His hands caught the sides of her lace

panties and dragged them down her silken legs. He rolled aside long enough to glide open the zipper of his slacks and ease them over his own hips.

Once they were both free of restrictive clothing, he knelt over her. Her eyes were golden, hot with need. Royce nearly groaned just looking at her, just feeling the heat radiating from her smooth ivory skin.

She raised her hand to his face, her fingertips grazing his cheekbone. "Love me," she whispered. "Just love me."

Her words, her touch were all the inducement Royce needed. He positioned himself over her, using his thighs to part hers. She opened to him without reserve, without restraint.

By all that was holy, Royce didn't know where he found the strength to go slowly, to linger, prolonging the moment. Her eyes held his as he pushed forward, gliding the throbbing, aching staff of his manhood into her.

If he were ever going to die from pleasure, it would have been at that moment. Catherine was ready for him, waiting for him, so sweet and hot and moist, Royce knew in a heartbeat that he dare not move.

His eyes returned to hers, which were half-closed as she, too, drank in the exquisite tumult. After giving her a moment to adjust to him,

Royce continued easing himself into her until she had taken in all of him.

Breathing hard, Catherine raised her knees and bucked beneath him. Royce groaned aloud as a flash of white-hot pleasure shot through him. Unable to endure much more, he pushed forward and was nearly consumed with the second wave of moist, hot bliss. When his eyes connected with Catherine, he noted that she was biting hard into her lower lip.

"I'm hurting you?" He didn't know if her reaction was one of pleasure or pain.

"No…oh, no," she whispered. "I never knew anything could feel this good."

"This is only the beginning," he promised. He closed his eyes in order to savor every sensation, drink in every fiery aspect of their lovemaking.

He honestly meant to go slow. He had to, he felt, in order to fully appreciate the magic between them. But once he started to rotate his hips, he was lost. Lost in pleasure. Lost in the storm, but he wasn't alone. Catherine clung to him, answering each bold thrust with one of her own.

It was a storm. One of need. One of fury and frenzy. It came on quickly, with such intensity that Royce was pitched from one world to another until he realized there was no slow-ing down, no going back. No stopping. Not for heaven, not for hell. For pain or for pleasure.

His climax came as a searing completion, far too quickly to suit Royce. He didn't want it to end, not now. Not so soon.

Catherine's labored breathing matched his own, and the sound of it was the only thing that shattered the silence as they both burned in the wake of the sweetest tempest Royce had ever known.

Royce woke around three to the sounds of Catherine singing. She was taking a shower. In the middle of the night no less.

Grinning, he rolled onto his back and raised his arms, cupped his head beneath his hands. They'd made love twice and then fallen into an exhausted sleep. The last thing Royce remembered was Catherine snuggling close to him, berating the fact she had yet to put on the special lace nightie she'd bought for their wedding night.

She came out of the bathroom and was bent over, briskly rubbing a towel over her wet hair. When she raised her head, she noted that Royce was lying in bed, watching her. Something he was sure she'd enjoy doing for many more years yet to come.

"I didn't wake you, did I?"

"As a matter of fact, you did." She had on the skimpiest nightie he'd ever seen. Although he was exhausted and physically drained, seeing her in that slip of black lace seriously threatened his composure.

"I apologize. I guess I shouldn't have started singing, but I just couldn't help myself…I don't know when I've been so happy. I don't think I ever want to leave this room."

Royce was thinking much along those same lines himself. He held out his arms. "Come here, woman."

Surprised, she glanced toward the bathroom. "I was going to blow-dry my hair."

"Later. You woke me, and there's a penance to be paid."

"But, Royce, it's the middle of the night. We've already…you know…several times."

"Come here." He grew impatient waiting for her. He rolled off the bed, walked over to where she was standing and removed the towel from her head, letting it fall to the carpet. He threaded her wet hair through his splayed fingers, cherishing the feel of her, so warm and moist. That caused him to think of other places on her delectable body that were warm and moist, too.

"What are you doing?"

"What am I doing now or what do I intend

to do later?" he asked, wiggling his eyebrows provocatively.

"We've already done everything there is to do," she announced primly.

"Is that a fact." He kissed her, sweeping his mouth across hers and giving her a taste of his tongue.

"Well, maybe not everything," she amended. He nibbled his way across her jaw to her earlobe and whispered seductive promises to her. He smiled, loving it when she responded with a sharp gasp.

"Royce… Why that's indecent."

"Oh, really." He kissed her a second time, sliding his tongue across the parted seam of her lips. Once more he captured the lobe of her ear between his teeth and sucked lightly. Then he whispered what he intended to do to her in a very short while.

"Royce!" Her eyes went wide. He loved watching her cheeks turn a fetching shade of pink.

Royce couldn't help it, he laughed. "And not just once, either. I have a lot of time to make up for, and you, my dear, sweet wife, have fallen right into my hands."

"But I…oh, Royce," she moaned as he traced a row of moist kisses across her face until he found her lips. The kiss was wet and wild. Wild and sweet.

His hands were busy trying to figure out how to take off the flimsy black nightie she wore. He eased the satin straps down her shoulders. She worked her arms free for him until he could remove the top completely, liberating her luscious breasts. He slid his palms over their fullness. Up and down, savoring her softness. Her femininity.

Unable to wait a moment longer, he lifted her into his arms and carried her to the bed, pressing her into the mattress. His body followed, covering hers. Instinctively she opened to him, and he entered her in one swift movement.

Catherine moaned.

Royce sighed.

Then the storm took over and they moved as one to hold back the torrent, or perhaps to bring it on—Royce didn't know which. The world went spinning out of control, a hurricane of wild need that consumed them both.

Catherine woke slowly. A serene smile lifted the corners of her mouth, and she rolled onto her back and raised her arms high above her head, as content as Sambo stretching after taking a long nap in the sunlight. Instinctively she rolled onto her side, seeking the warmth and comfort of Royce's body.

The space beside her was empty, however. And cold. Her eyes opened, and sadness settled over her, blocking out the early-morning sunlight.

They'd spent less than five nights together. Five nights out of a lifetime, and she continued to search for him. At night she tossed restlessly in her sleep, seeking his warmth, seeking his strength. No one had warned her how dangerously addictive it was to sleep with a husband.

Royce and Kelly were in Norfolk and had been for two weeks. They communicated often. Letters arrived nearly every day, and their phone bill rivaled the defense budget. Yet Catherine found the grating loneliness inescapable.

She didn't know which was worse. Loving Royce and being forced to hide the way she felt behind a deluge of Navy regulations or being married to him and separated by two thousand endless miles.

It wouldn't be any worse if Royce were stationed aboard one of the submarines, at least that was what she told herself. They'd be apart for months on end. Just the way they were now.

Before he and Kelly had left for Norfolk, they'd made plans for Catherine to join them over the Christmas holidays. That wasn't so long to wait.

A few days. Surely she could hold on to her peace of mind for a few more days, especially when they were said to be the shortest days of the year.

Catherine did manage to survive, but just barely. Royce and Kelly were waiting for her at the airport when her plane touched down. The minute Kelly saw her, she flew into Catherine's arms, hugging her as though it had been years since they'd last seen each other.

"Oh, Catherine, I'm so glad you're here."

Catherine was glad, too. She raised her head, and her eyes connected with Royce's. His were warm and welcoming. She stepped into his embrace and squeezed tight.

"We've got everything ready for you," Kelly told her excitedly. "Dad and I worked real hard putting up the Christmas tree and wrapping presents. I even helped him clean the kitchen and everything."

"Thank you sweetheart. I appreciate it so much." She gave the ten-year-old a second bear hug. She'd missed Royce's daughter, too, more than she'd thought possible.

"Can we do my nails again?" Kelly asked,

holding out her hands for a visual inspection. "They look just wretched, don't they?"

"Of course we'll both work on our nails."

"Shopping, too. Dad's simply impossible, but then he always was."

Royce collected her luggage and led the way through the terminal to the parking garage. The ride into Norfolk took only a few minutes. The weather had cooperated beautifully, and the sky was crisp and clear with a sprinkling of stars scattered boldly across the horizon of black velvet.

The colonial house was exactly as Royce had described. Catherine liked it immediately and felt its welcome the minute she walked through the wreath-covered door.

"Did you miss me?" Kelly asked, clinging to Catherine's arm. "Because I sure missed you," Kelly said, and then her voice lowered. "Dad missed you, too."

"Oh, sweetheart, I missed you both so much."

"What about..." Kelly paused and darted a look toward her father. Once more she lowered her voice several decibels. "You know."

Catherine didn't know. "What?"

Losing patience, Kelly clenched her fists against her hipbones. "A baby. Are you pregnant yet, or not?"

"Not," Royce informed his daughter crisply.

"Not," Catherine echoed in a far more gentle tone. Unfortunately. Catherine had given a good deal of thought to the idea of them adding to their family. True, Kelly wanting, or rather demanding a baby sister, had been the catalyst, but when Catherine analyzed it, she had to admit the ten-year-old had a valid point. Royce was already in his late thirties, and she was at the age when all the internal female workings were at their peak.

Catherine wasn't keen about going through a pregnancy without Royce being close to love and pamper her during the discomforts she was likely to encounter. Yet Navy officers through the ages had suffered no less. She wasn't an exception.

Beyond all the other token reasons, Catherine longed for Royce's child. The matter had been on her mind every minute that she'd been separated from Royce these past two weeks. She might be rushing matters, but the idea strongly appealed to her. She planned to approach her husband about the subject during this brief visit. If everything went according to schedule, this might well be a bonus Christmas.

Kelly chatted for the next hour, telling Catherine all about her school and her new friends. Catherine had heard it all before, but gave her rapt attention to Kelly while Royce brewed hot-buttered rums.

"All I get is hot butter," Kelly said with a grimace when Royce delivered the steaming drinks.

"The only reason you get that is so you'll go up to bed the way you promised."

"Dad!" Kelly exclaimed. "It's Christmas Eve's eve. You don't honestly expect me to go to bed at the regular time, do you?"

"It's two hours past your bedtime already," he reminded her. "Now drink up and hit the sack."

"You just want time alone with Catherine," the youngster accused as she sipped from the edge of her mug. "But," she added with an expressive sigh, "I can understand. People in love need that."

"Thank you, Dear Abby," Royce teased. "Now scoot."

Kelly took one last sip of her drink, then set it on the counter. She gave both Royce and Catherine hugs, then dutifully marched up the stairs.

Now that Catherine was alone with her husband, she watched as he stood and turned out the lamps until the only light illuminating the room came from the ones blinking on the Christmas tree. Although dim, the beautifully decorated tree gave off a soft glare, enough for her to realize Royce was studying her. His cobalt-blue eyes said all sorts of things that words could never express. They told her how much he'd missed her and how he woke each morning searching for her. He'd been left to confront a cold empty space just the way she had. His eyes also told her how much he needed her. Physically. Emotionally. Mentally. Every which way there was to need a woman, he needed her.

Slowly, never taking his eyes from her, he removed the steaming mug from her hands, setting it aside. He reached for her then, gently taking her into his arms and kissing her with a hunger that told her his nights had been as achingly lonesome as her own. While his mouth was hotly claiming hers, he was working at opening her blouse and bra. He was so eager to love her, his hands shook.

"Royce," she pleaded, "the bedroom's upstairs."

"We can't, at least not yet," he argued. "Kelly won't be asleep."

"But she might come down here."

"She won't. I promise." His voice was a low growl, heavy with impatience.

"Don't you think we should wait?"

"I can't. Not a second longer. Feel me." He grabbed hold of her wrist and boldly pressed it to him. "I need you," he said, his voice strained as she took the initiative and moved her open palm back and forth.

"I need you, too," she returned in a husky murmur, closing her eyes to the loving way in which he sought her breasts, lifting them, scoring the undersides with his thumbs. If she hadn't been so fascinated with touching him, with receiving his touch, she would have been rushing to remove her clothes.

"I've thought of nothing else but this from the moment we parted."

"Oh...yes."

"I want you so damn much I can't think straight."

"Me, too."

"I want you more than I ever believed it was possible to want another human being."

"You know what I want?" She didn't wait for him to answer. "I want you to stop talking about wanting me, and hurry up and carry me to bed so we can make love."

He laughed, and Catherine swore it was the most wonderful, melodious sound in the world. He reached her hand and hurried her up the stairs. They tiptoed past Kelly's bedroom with Catherine clenching her blouse closed.

The instant they were alone, his mouth sought hers in a fierce kiss that sent her senses reeling.

The winds of their passion were building,

gaining momentum. Royce scooped her into the shelter of his arms and pressed her against the mattress. Then, without hesitation, he removed her clothes with a few agile movements.

Catherine raised her arms, waiting to curl them around his neck as he quickly removed his own clothing.

"Come here, husband," she whispered wantonly. "Let me show you exactly how much I missed you...."

Catherine woke several hours later. She was in bed with Royce cuddling her spoon fashion as though they'd been sleeping together for years. He really was a romantic creature, but it would have embarrassed him had she told him so.

The flight across the country had exhausted her. A smile scooted across her lips. Perhaps it had, but not nearly as much as the session with her husband.

Royce rolled onto his back, giving her the opportunity to study him in the dim moonlight. His features were relaxed in slumber, and the musky scent of their lovemaking lingered. Her heart felt full, open wide to receive all the love he had to give her. It was a good feeling.

"Catherine?"

"Did I wake you?"

"Yes," he said, yawning, "and you know the penalty."

"Oh, Royce," she whispered, grinning, then gave an exaggerated sigh. "Not again."

"Oh, yes…'again' as you so eloquently put it."

Elevating her head, she leaned over and kissed him gently. "Can we have a talk first?"

"Must we?"

"Yes." Her lips briefly touched his. "Please."

"This sounds serious."

She kissed him again, cherishing the taste of him.

His hands held her face away from his. "Either we talk or we kiss. We can't do both."

"All right. One kiss and then we talk. Seriously." His hands were in her hair, unerringly directing her mouth to his for an intimate kiss that was slow and familiar.

"Enough," he whispered, dragging his mouth from her. "Now talk."

"Royce," she said, drawing in a deep breath. "What would you think if I were to become pregnant?"

The air went cold and still. "Are you?"

"No, but I'd like to be."

His eyes closed briefly as though he were greatly relieved. "Not a good idea."

"Why not?" His attitude stung more than she

ever thought it would. She expected some hesitation on his part, but nothing like this.

"As long as you're in the Navy there won't be any children for us. I thought you understood that."

Thirteen

"What do you mean?" Catherine demanded, sitting up in the bed and grabbing the sheet by her fists to cover her bare breasts.

"Exactly what I said." Royce was frowning heavily. "There won't be any children for us as long as you're in the Navy. I thought you understood that."

"I want to know when the hell I agreed to that." She was angry, but damn it all, she couldn't help it. How arrogant. How highhanded of him. She was the one who was willing to go through with the pregnancy. The one who'd offered to balance both her career and a family. It was what she wanted, what she'd planned all along. She'd swallow a gallon of seawater before she'd ever agree to no children.

"We talked about it before we were married," Royce announced coolly.

"The hell we did."

"Catherine, think about it. We had several serious discussions about what we would do if you weren't transferred to Norfolk with me. Remember?" His patience was as grating as his words.

Various conversations they'd had about her transferring did come to mind, and she reluctantly nodded. "Yes, but I certainly don't remember us saying anything about children."

"Trust me, we did."

"Wrong," she returned heatedly. "You're making the whole thing up...I would never have agreed to it. I want a baby, I've always wanted a baby. Two babies." That should really outrage him. Imagine her being greedy enough to want more than one!

An ironic grin quirked the edges of his mouth. "Fine, if that's what you want, we'll have three or four children. More if you want."

"Good." Apparently he wasn't going to make as much of a fuss over this as she'd originally thought. The outrage slowly drained out of her.

"We'll work hard on getting you pregnant," Royce added purposefully, "just as soon as you resign your commission."

"What?" Catherine was on her knees, the protective shield covering her nakedness long forgotten. She was so furious, she leaped to her feet and started traipsing across the mattress in giant steps. Leaping onto the carpet, she searched for something to cover herself with and grabbed a shirt of Royce's that was hanging in the closet. She jerked it so hard the hanger clattered to the floor.

It didn't help matters to have Royce casually sitting up in bed, propped against two fat pillows. "Is there a problem with that?"

"You're damn right there is."

"Then why don't we sit down like two civilized people and discuss this rationally."

"Because," she cried, hands braced on her hips, "I'm too damn mad. I never dreamed...not once that you'd do something like this."

"Catherine, if you'd cool off for a moment we could talk this over rationally."

"I'm cool," she shouted, holding back her hair with both hands. "Answer me one thing."

"All right."

"Do you want a baby?" The whole world seemed to stop. It was as though their marriage, indeed their relationship, hung on a delicate balance, weighed by his answer.

"Yes," he whispered with enough feeling to convince her it was true. "I've tried to tell myself it didn't matter. That I'd leave everything up to you, but damn it, yes, I would like another child." He said it almost as if he were admitting to a weakness.

Catherine was so grateful, her knees weakened. "Oh, Royce, I do, too, so much."

"Apparently the communication between us isn't as good as I'd thought."

"Why are we arguing?" she asked softly.

He grinned. "I don't know. Damn it, Catherine, I love you too much to fight with you."

"I'm glad to hear that." The long-sleeved shirt she'd so hastily donned silently slipped to the floor. With an unhurried ease, she walked over to the side of the bed, her head held high and proud. "As far as I'm concerned the sooner we make a baby the better, don't you think?"

"Catherine?" Royce sounded unsure, which wasn't like him.

"I want to make love." She sat on the edge of the mattress and sought his mouth, kissing him so lightly that their lips barely touched.

Royce groaned, grabbed her by the hair and plunged his tongue deeply into the moist hollow of her mouth. The kiss was so hot it threatened to blister them both.

"We need to finish our talk first," he murmured breathlessly, but even while he was speaking, he was kissing her. He groaned and shook his head. "Catherine…we can't do this."

"Later… We'll talk later."

"I don't think that would be a good idea." He firmly grabbed hold of both her wrists in an attempt to push her back, but the maneuver didn't work. Instead of fighting, she leaned into him, taking full advantage of the fact his hands were occupied. Murmuring words of love and sexual need, she seduced him. Whispering to him between kisses, she told him all the things she planned to do for him. All the things they'd do for each other.

"Catherine…" He didn't sound nearly so insistent as before. "I don't…we need to talk before we do anything…first."

"If that's what you really want," she whispered, taking his earlobe between her teeth and biting lightly. "Touch me," she pleaded softly. "Oh, Royce…I need you so much."

His hold on her wrist slackened. "Catherine, I don't think it would be a good idea—"

"I do…" She was kneeling over him, her thighs spread wide, anticipating the contact, knowing it would play havoc with them both. This was what she wanted, what she needed.

Royce hesitated; his face was hard, his eyes closed, blocking her out, because that was the only way he had of resisting her. The power she felt was strong enough to intoxicate her.

Neither moved. Neither breathed. The pleasure was too intense for either. There was no beginning. No end. The pleasure, once it started, only grew better. The joy burst forth in Catherine's heart until it filled every ounce, every pore of her being.

Joy. Pleasure. The tenderness so sweet it was violent. The beauty of their lovemaking transcending anything she had ever experienced.

When they'd finished, Royce cradled her in his arms. Neither spoke. After what seemed like forever, Royce reached for the blankets, covering them both. His arms held her close, nestling her head against his hard chest. He kissed the crown of her head, and whispered that they would talk in the morning.

Morning. Catherine's eyes slowly drifted open, and she snuggled against Royce's cozy warmth. He must have sensed that she was awake, because he ran his hand over the top of her head, smoothing her hair.

"Are you going to argue with me again?" he whispered.

"That depends on how unreasonable you intend on being," she said, rolling onto her back and arching her body, yawning. "I'm…sorry about last night." She was embarrassed now at the brazen way in which she'd come at him. Using their physical need for each other as a weapon to twist his will was not a tactic she'd ever intended to employ. But he'd made her so furious, she hadn't been thinking properly.

"I want a child, Royce," she told him, her voice low and determined.

"It's not a problem," he assured her, "as long as you're out of the Navy."

His stubbornness stunned her. "Why should I be the one to give up my commission?" she asked, in what she hoped was a reasonable tone. Her emotions were pitching around like a small rowboat upon a stormy ocean. The waves of righteousness slapped roughly against the sides. It was all so unfair. She had to make Royce understand that.

"How about if you give up your commission first?" she offered, hoping he'd see the foolishness of his logic.

He didn't answer her right away. "You agreed before we were married. We discussed it and—"

"We didn't," she denied vehemently.

"…and you chose to stay in the Navy," Royce finished as though she'd never spoken. "Obviously it wasn't as clear as I'd thought it was, and that's unfortunate, but the fact remains…"

"I'm going to have a child, Royce, and I'm going to be the best mother you ever saw. I'm going to prove to you that I can also be a damn good lieutenant commander as well—"

"No." His voice was gruff and angry.

"Why do I have to be the one to resign?" She

wasn't being flippant this time, but she honestly wanted to know.

"Because a child deserves a mother."

"What about a father?"

"One of us has to accept the majority of the responsibility."

"We can't share the duty?"

"No," he argued, more heatedly this time.

"Why are you being so stubborn about this?" she demanded. Royce might be a lot of things, but she'd always found him to be fair.

"Because Sandy—"

"Now just a minute," Catherine said, struggling into a sitting position. She narrowed her eyes as she stared down on him. "Get this straight right now, Royce Nyland. I refuse to be compared with your first wife. I'm not Sandy, and I won't have you holding me up to her." She climbed off the bed and stalked across the room, heading for the bathroom to take a long hot shower and cool off her indignation. She paused, her hand on the doorknob. "There's something you should know." She didn't dare look at him. "I woke up…in the middle of the night last night…" She wasn't proud of this and refused to turn around and look at him as she admitted what she'd done.

"And what?" Royce demanded.

"I...I flushed my birth control pills down the toilet."

She heard his muffled curse as she stepped inside the bathroom.

The shower was running, and Catherine was standing under the stinging spray when the door was thrust open and Royce stepped inside.

"What the hell did you do that for?" He didn't need to explain what he was asking about.

"Because." Catherine was well aware her answer didn't make sense.

"It won't make a whole lot of difference. All I have to do is make a trip to the drugstore."

"Fine. Do it." She reached for the bar of soap and lathered the washcloth. "I'm tired of having everything rest on my shoulders. It's time for someone else to take responsibility."

Royce frowned at that. The water pelted down around him, splashing against the sides of the cubicle. "I'm not going to argue with you. These days are too precious to spend fighting. Even if we were to agree about you getting pregnant, it's too soon. Let's wait a year and talk about it then. A lot could change in that time. There's no need for either of us to get caught up in our disagreements when there's so much we do agree on."

He shouldn't make this much sense. It should be black-and-white. Cut-and-dried.

His hand was under her chin. "I love you,

Catherine, I'd much rather be making love to you than standing here debating a subject I assumed was closed." He leaned forward and gently brushed moist lips over hers.

Heaven help her, but she couldn't resist him. Not like this. She stood on her tiptoes and looped her arms around his neck, easing her softness against his hard, lean strength. Steam fogged the windows and mirrors, but Catherine was convinced it had nothing to do with the hot spray of water and everything to do with the way Royce was kissing her.

As it happened, the water turned cold a whole lot sooner than either of them did.

Catherine was frying bacon for Kelly's breakfast when Royce came bolting down the stairs. He grabbed his jacket and was heading toward the front door when Kelly stopped him.

"Where're you going, Dad?"

He hesitated and cast a dark frown in Catherine's direction. "Shopping."

"It's too early in the morning for anything to be open," Kelly informed him with perfect logic.

"A drugstore will be," he muttered, and moved out the front door, slamming it behind him.

Smiling contentedly to herself, Catherine continued to fry the bacon.

It wasn't supposed to happen like this, Catherine told herself a month later. A woman didn't flush her birth control pills down the toilet one minute and, bingo, turn up pregnant the next. This was one for the record books. Something like this was supposed to take weeks. Months.

Not seconds.

As far as Catherine could figure it out, she was more fertile than the Napa Valley.

She didn't know what she was going to tell Royce. Or when. Not soon, she decided. This pregnancy was something that would demand diplomacy and tact. Good grief, only a handful of people in Bangor even knew she was married.

If only she weren't so thrilled about it. So excited. Of course being separated the way they were, she might even be able to have the baby without Royce knowing.

But that was ridiculous. He was the father. He deserved to know. Kelly deserved to know.

She waited all day for his phone call, deciding to play it by ear. At precisely six, her time, just after she'd poured herself a cup of coffee, the phone rang.

She grabbed it off the hook, holding the receiver tight against her ear. She reminded herself that she was an accomplished attorney who knew her way around the courtroom. She could argue with the best of them. Her arguments had swayed more than one judge. All she needed to do was remain collected and poised. This child, although unexpected, was a welcome gift. Once Royce saw things from her point of view, he'd change his mind. He didn't have any choice. The deed was done.

"Catherine?"

"Hi," she answered cheerfully. "How are you? How's Kelly? Not much happening around here except that the strip turned blue." Catherine couldn't believe she'd blurted it out like that, although it was unlikely that Royce knew she was referring to the home pregnancy kit she'd picked up at the pharmacy.

"What are you talking about?"

"Oh, nothing. Just a bit of local humor. Are you missing me?"

"You know I am." His words were low and seductive.

They talked for a half hour, the longest thirty minutes of Catherine's life. The minute they were finished, she rushed into the bathroom and hung her head over the toilet. She was never going to be able to pull this off. Royce would guess by the end of the week. She didn't know what would infuriate him more, the fact she hadn't told him right away or that she was pregnant in the first place.

Catherine gained two important lessons from her thirty-minute conversation with Royce. First, that she would need to confide in someone, and second, she wasn't going to be able to drink coffee for the next nine months.

"Hi, Mom," Catherine greeted.

"Sweetheart, what's wrong?"

"How did you know anything was?"

"You mean other than the fact you're phoning and it's past midnight? Don't worry, I wasn't asleep. Norman went to bed hours ago, but I'm up reading one of Mary Higgins Clark's mysteries."

"Midnight. I didn't realize it was that late."

"You always call late when you're upset."

Catherine didn't realize that, either. "Say, Mom, what would you say if I told you the strip turned blue?"

The pause was only slight. "Is this a trick question?"

"No...I'm dead serious."

"A strip turned blue. I don't know, sweetheart, probably that you should see a doctor."

"Right answer," she said on the tail of a

breathy sigh. "Now comes the difficult part. Can you guess why I need a doctor?"

Again there was a semi-lengthy pause. "I'd say it was because you were pregnant, but I know that's not the case."

"Wrong answer."

"You mean...Catherine, do you honestly mean to tell me you and Royce are... But you've only been married a short while, and he's in Virginia and you're in Washington state. Honey, how did it happen?"

"You want me to explain it to you?" Catherine asked incredulously.

"You know what I mean." Catherine could almost see her mother blushing.

"Christmas," Catherine whispered.

"You don't sound like you're sure you're pleased about this."

"I'm thrilled, Mom, honest I am."

"Are you going to leave the Navy?"

"No!"

"But, Catherine, can't you see how impossible it will be? You and Royce live two thousand miles apart. A child deserves to know his father."

"Royce will see the baby."

Her mother must have sensed the argument brewing just below the surface of Catherine's stubborn pride, because she diplomatically changed the subject.

"I'm going to tell you something I never have before," Marilyn said softly, gently. "You, my darling daughter, were a surprise."

"I was?"

"Actually, you were more of a shock."

Catherine grinned. Her sense of timing never had gotten straightened out, it seemed.

"Your father and I were in college. Young. Idealistic. Foolish."

"Do you mean to tell me you and Dad *had* to get married?"

"No, but as best as I can figure you were born nine months and one day after our wedding. I didn't know how I was going to tell your father. As it turned out, he was delighted. I was crying—the hormones really did a trick on me. I'll never forget how gentle he was, how pleased. It was as though I were the only woman in the world who'd ever endured a pregnancy." Her mother paused, and Catherine could hear the slight quaver in her voice.

"In those days the father wasn't often allowed in the delivery room. But Andy refused to leave me. For a minute there I thought he and the doctor were going to come to blows."

Catherine enjoyed hearing these loving details about her father. Her gaze rested tenderly on the fading color photograph that rested atop her mantel.

"When you were born, I was afraid he would be disappointed with a daughter. But not Andy. The delivery room nurse placed you in his arms, and he sat beside me and wept for joy.

"After they wheeled me into the recovery room, I was exhausted and fell asleep. But Andy was too excited to stand still. The nurses told me he dragged everyone from the janitor to the hospital administrator up to the nursery to take a look at you. Not once did he regret that I'd become pregnant so soon." Her mother paused, and Catherine could hear her voice tremble with soft emotion.

"I love hearing stories about him," Catherine admitted, discovering she was close to tears herself, which probably meant this pregnancy was going to play havoc with her emotions.

"Royce doesn't know yet, does he?" her mother pried softly.

"No."

"When exactly do you plan to tell him?"

"Next year when it's time to figure our income taxes?"

Her mother's laughter echoed softly over the long-distance line. "Oh, Catherine, you remind me so much of myself, and so much of your father. Royce is a good man, I don't think you have a thing to worry about."

They spoke for a few minutes more, and then Catherine hung up. Slowly, thoughtfully, she walked over to the fireplace and gently ran her finger along the top of her father's picture. It was something she did often when she needed to feel close to him. She prayed her mother was right and that Royce would be thrilled. Her gaze rested on her father's handsome features. A lone tear streaked her face as she regretted once again her inability to remember him.

Royce was weary as he drove down the maple-lined street and pulled into his driveway. He missed Catherine. It had been nearly three months since he'd last seen her, and it could well be another three before he did again. He tried not to think about it.

They were close, as close as any two married people could be that were separated by the width of an entire country. If anything troubled him it was the fact she was so content with their arrangement. They talked two times a week and wrote nearly every day. Only on rare occasions did Catherine reveal any regrets on their being so far removed from each other.

Not so with Royce. He wanted his wife with him. If he was being selfish, inconsiderate, then so be it. The nights were lonely. Friday nights were always the worst. Kelly usually spent it with a friend, which left him to fend for himself. He was pleased his daughter had such an active social life; his, however, was wrapped around a woman two thousand miles away.

He really knew how to pick them, he mused darkly. Career women. First Sandy and now Catherine, both so eager to make a place in their chosen profession.... No, he wasn't going to dwell on it. He'd done that too much lately. He'd gone into this marriage with his eyes wide open. From the first he'd known how important the Navy was to Catherine. He'd married her still, loving her enough to place a distant second in her life if that was all she was willing to give him.

His life was good. He had only a few complaints. He liked Virginia much better than he ever expected he would. He enjoyed his job, and over the past few months had developed several interests. He wasn't much into hobbies—at least he hadn't been until he married Catherine. Now he had to find something to fill the time or go crazy thinking about how much he missed her.

He just wished there was some way he could get her transferred out to the East Coast. Even if she were stationed in Florida, it would be a whole lot closer than Washington state.

The lights were on in the house, and Royce was trying to remember if Kelly was going to be home or not. Home, he guessed.

He opened the front door and removed his jacket and hung it in the hall closet. Someone was cooking in the kitchen. Whatever it was it smelled like heaven. Royce was going to have to say something to Kelly about fixing dinner. She was too young to be attempting it without adult supervision.

"Kelly?" He paused to sort through the mail.

"I'm in the kitchen, Dad." She sounded downright pleased about something. Probably that she'd managed to cook his dinner without burning down the house.

"What smells so good?"

"Yankee pot roast, mashed potatoes, steamed baby carrots and fresh-baked apple pie."

The mail dropped out of Royce's hands as he slowly turned around. He was dreaming. He had to be, because it was Catherine's honey-sweet voice that was talking to him and not Kelly's. She stood in the kitchen doorway, a towel tucked into the waistband of her jeans, holding a wooden spoon in one hand.

"Catherine?" He was almost afraid to reach for her for fear she'd vanish into thin air. Either real or imaginary, he had to hold her. Two steps later, and she was in his arms.

He closed his eyes and breathed in the warm, familiar fragrance of her, intoxicated within seconds. His arms were wrapped around her so tightly that he'd lifted her half off the floor without even realizing it.

"Are you surprised?" Kelly asked.

"You knew?" He couldn't believe that she'd managed to keep it a secret from him.

"Only since yesterday."

He kissed Catherine with a hunger that quickly stirred awake dormant fires. "How long can you stay?" Mentally he was tabulating how many times they could make love in three days.

"How long do you want me for?"

A lifetime! Fifty years or whichever came first. "How long have you got?" No use aiming for the stars. He'd take what he could get and be damned grateful.

"A while." She kissed him, tantalizing him with the tip of her tongue, and then casually sauntered back to the stove.

"A while," Royce repeated, not understanding.

"Now?" Kelly demanded, looking up at Catherine.

Catherine nodded mysteriously. Royce's daughter held up her two hands. "Ten minutes," she said. "That's all the time I'm giving you."

"It shouldn't even take that long," Catherine assured her.

Kelly was gone in a flash, racing up the stairs.

"Ten minutes," Royce repeated once Kelly was out of the room. "Honey, I don't know what you've got in mind, but I'd appreciate a bit more leeway than ten minutes."

"I want you to read something." She walked over to the table and handed him an official-looking envelope.

Royce stared at it for several moments, not knowing what to think.

"And while I've got your attention, I think you should know we killed a rabbit."

"What?" The woman had become a loony tune. A three-month separation had driven her over the edge. He knew it had him, so it shouldn't come as any big surprise.

"Actually I don't think it's officially a rabbit these days."

"Woman, what are you talking about?"

"You mean you honestly don't know?" He clearly seemed to not know.

He wouldn't be standing there with his mouth open, looking like a fish out of water if he did. "I don't have a clue," he admitted reluctantly.

"We're pregnant."

Royce shook his head, convinced she was playing a practical joke on him.

"It's true, Royce." Her eyes met his, shyly, as though she were honestly afraid of his reaction. She was studying him closely, judging his response, watching him for any signs of emotion.

Royce felt the sudden need to sit down. "When?"

"As-s best I can figure, sometime over Christmas. My guess was that morning…in the shower."

He nodded. He felt too numb to do much of anything else. He started figuring dates. It had happened at Christmas, and they were already into the second week of March.

"But that was…"

"A few months ago now," she finished for him.

"You're three months pregnant?" She'd kept it a secret for all those months.

She nodded. "Aren't you going to say anything? Oh, Royce, please don't keep me in suspense any longer. Are you happy?"

He struggled for words, but the emotions had jammed in his throat. He swallowed and slowed his breath before nodding. "Yes." He reached for her, taking her by the hips and drawing her to him. He flattened his hand over her stomach and closed his eyes. It was impossible for him to speak.

"Read the letter," she whispered, and tears

slipped from the corners of her eyes and ran unrestrained down her cheeks. She brushed them aside. "Don't worry, I'm terribly emotional these days. I start weeping at the drop of a hat, but the doctor said it wasn't anything to be concerned about."

Royce withdrew the paper from inside the envelope. He scanned the contents twice, certain there was some misunderstanding.

"You're leaving the Navy?" he asked, his voice incredulous.

"Yes, but I'm still in the Reserves."

"Why?" After all her arguments about keeping her commission, he couldn't believe that she'd voluntarily give it up.

Catherine's arms circled his neck, and she lowered herself onto his lap. "Because I finally figured out why the Navy was so important for me."

Royce stared up at her, not understanding.

"I was searching to know my father, looking to find him in Navy life... I know it all sounds crazy, but having no memory of him has troubled me for years. Hanging on to the Navy, especially now, was like grasping at straws, because I wanted to find something about him to hang on to."

"But what changed your mind?"

"Our baby. I realized I could do it. Raise our

child and everything else when we were so far apart. Then it dawned on me how silly I was being, grasping to find my own father and denying my own child the privilege."

Royce kissed her, worshipping her with his mouth, loving her until they were both trembling.

"Have you told him yet?" Kelly demanded from the top of the stairs.

"She told me," Royce answered.

Kelly raced down. "What do you think, Dad?"

He grinned and held out his hand to his daughter, bringing her into the circle of their love. It was more than he ever dreamed, more than he deserved. Taking Catherine's hand, he pressed her fingertips to his lips. Their eyes held, and in hers Royce saw the warm promise of tomorrow.

Epilogue

Royce was whistling a catchy tune when he pulled into the driveway and turned off the engine. The station wagon was parked alongside of his black Porsche, a baby seat strapped in the rear seat.

Andy was fast outgrowing the padded chair, which worked out well since Jenny would soon be needing it. His three-month-old daughter was growing like a weed.

Pushing a tricycle out of the way, Royce opened the front door and hung his hat and jacket on the brass coatrack. "I'm home."

Four-year-old Andy let out a cry of glee and came tearing around the corner at top speed. Royce swept his son high above his head and hugged him close.

"How's Daddy's little man? Did you help your mother today by being a good boy?"

"Aye, aye, sir." Andrew Royce Nyland saluted

sharply, then squirmed, wanting back down. The minute his feet hit the floor, Andy was back to whatever it was that had captured his attention in the first place.

"Royce," Catherine greeted, coming into the entryway, holding their daughter. A smile came automatically to his lips. It never ceased to amaze him, after all these years, all this time, how his heart quickened at the sight of her. She was in a blue business suit with a fancy silk blouse, and Royce vaguely remembered her telling him she'd had to go into the office later than usual. He was proud of the way Catherine had found a position in a prestigious law firm. Proud of her for showing him it was possible to mix a career with a family. She worked three days a week now, but when the time was right, she would eventually take on a forty-hour week. Frankly, Royce felt his wife had something of an advantage over other attorneys. She was so damn beautiful and intelligent he couldn't see a jury in the land disagreeing with her.

"Oh, Royce, I'm glad you're home." Catherine paused to give him a quick but satisfying kiss, handing him Jenny. No sooner was his daughter in his arms, when Catherine was reaching for her coat.

"Where are you headed?"

She turned around and chastised him with a

smile. "I told you about the Navy wives meeting this evening, don't you remember?"

"Oh, right." Royce recalled nothing of the sort. He had trouble keeping track of his own schedule, let alone everyone else's.

"Kelly will be home within a half hour," Catherine informed him. "And she's bringing a young man home with her."

"A boy?"

"Royce, she's almost sixteen. This is important to her, so don't make a fuss. All she asks is that you give her a little privacy."

"Hey," he grumbled, reaching for his wife. "How does she rate? If anyone deserves a little privacy, it's us." He kissed her along the side of the neck, savoring her special fragrance. "What time are you going to be home?"

"Not late," she promised, rubbing her mouth over his lips in a slow, erotic exercise. "I promise."

Royce reluctantly released her. "Good, because I've got plans for tonight."

"You've got plans for every night," she teased, "which is a good thing because if you didn't, I would have." She grabbed her purse, started for the front door and turned back around.

"Forget something?"

"Yes." She patted Jenny's sleeping brow and

then raised her mouth to his. The kiss was one for the record books. Teasing. Coaxing.

Royce felt his knees grow weak, and if it hadn't been for Jenny, he would have wrapped his arms around Catherine and hauled her up the stairs right then and there.

Catherine sighed and hesitantly broke away from him.

"What was that for?" he asked breathlessly.

"Just so you'd know how much I love you. How grateful I am that you were patient enough to allow me to come to my own decisions. About the Navy. About my joining the law firm. About having Jenny."

"I sincerely hope you intend on thanking me again later."

"You know I do." She grinned and started for the door. Royce turned toward the kitchen, whistling contentedly.

* * * * *

The ESSENTIAL COLLECTION

YES! Please send me the *Essential Collection by Debbie Macomber* in Larger Print. This collection begins with 3 FREE books and 2 FREE gifts in the first shipment, and more free gifts will follow! My books will arrive in 8 monthly shipments until I have the entire 51-book *Essential Collection by Debbie Macomber*. I will receive 2 or 3 FREE books in each shipment and I will pay just $4.99 U.S./$5.89 CDN. for each of the other 4 books in each shipment, plus $2.99 for shipping and handling. *If I decide to keep the entire collection, I'll have paid for only 32 books because 19 books are FREE! I understand that by accepting the 3 free books and gifts places me under no obligation to buy anything. I can always return a shipment and cancel at any time. My free books and gifts are mine to keep no matter what I decide.

261 HCN 1446   461 HCN 1446

Name	(PLEASE PRINT)

Address	Apt. #

City	State/Prov.	Zip/Postal Code

Signature (if under 18, a parent or guardian must sign)

Mail to the Harlequin® Reader Service:

IN U.S.A.: P.O. Box 1867, Buffalo, NY 14240-1867
IN CANADA: P.O. Box 609, Fort Erie, Ontario L2A 5X3

* Terms and prices subject to change without notice. Prices do not include applicable taxes. Sales tax applicable in N.Y. Canadian residents will be charged applicable taxes. This offer is limited to one order per household. All orders subject to approval. Credit or debit balances in a customer's account(s) may be offset by any other outstanding balance owed by or to the customer. Please allow 4 to 6 weeks for delivery. Offer available while quantities last. Offer not available to Quebec residents.

Your Privacy—The Harlequin® Reader Service is committed to protecting your privacy. Our Privacy Policy is available online at www.ReaderService.com or upon request from the Harlequin Reader Service.

We make a portion of our mailing list available to reputable third parties that offer products we believe may interest you. If you prefer that we not exchange your name with third parties, or if you wish to clarify or modify your communication preferences, please visit us at www.ReaderService.com/consumerschoice or write to us at Harlequin Reader Service Preference Service, P.O. Box 9062, Buffalo, NY 14269. Include your complete name and address.

Reader Service.com

Manage your account online!

- Review your order history
- Manage your payments
- Update your address

---

*We've designed
the Harlequin® Reader Service
website just for you.*

Enjoy all the features!

- Reader excerpts from any series
- Respond to mailings and special monthly offers
- Discover new series available to you
- Browse the Bonus Bucks catalog
- Share your feedback

Visit us at:
ReaderService.com